Five Nights at Freddy's
FAZBEAR FRIGHTS #7
THE CLIFFS

Five Nights at Freddy's

Fazbear Frights #7
THE CLIFFS

SCOTT CAWTHON
ELLEY COOPER
ANDREA WAGGENER

Scholastic Inc.

If you purchased this book without a cover, you should be aware that this book is stolen property. It was reported as "unsold and destroyed" to the publisher, and neither the author nor the publisher has received any payment for this "stripped book."

Copyright © 2021 by Scott Cawthon. All rights reserved.

Photo of TV static: © Klikk/Dreamstime

All rights reserved. Published by Scholastic Inc., *Publishers since 1920*. SCHOLASTIC and associated logos are trademarks and/or registered trademarks of Scholastic Inc.

The publisher does not have any control over and does not assume any responsibility for author or third-party websites or their content.

No part of this publication may be reproduced, stored in a retrieval system, or transmitted in any form or by any means, electronic, mechanical, photocopying, recording, or otherwise, without written permission of the publisher. For information regarding permission, write to Scholastic Inc., Attention: Permissions Department, 557 Broadway, New York, NY 10012.

This book is a work of fiction. Names, characters, places, and incidents are either the product of the author's imagination or are used fictitiously, and any resemblance to actual persons, living or dead, business establishments, events, or locales is entirely coincidental.

Library of Congress Cataloging-in-Publication Data available

ISBN 978-1-338-70391-7

10 9 8 7 6 5 4 3 2 1   21 22 23 24 25

Printed in the U.S.A.

First printing 2021 • Book design by Betsy Peterschmidt

TABLE OF CONTENTS

The Cliffs
by Elley Cooper........1

The Breaking Wheel
by Andrea Waggener....57

He Told Me Everything
by Elley Cooper.......135

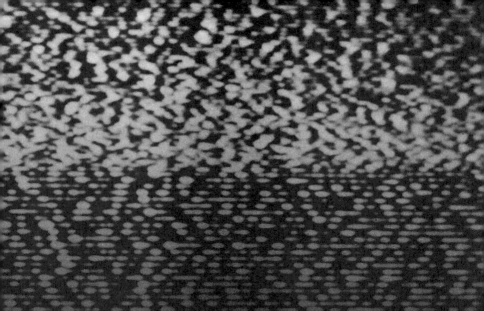

THE CLIFFS

Tyler knocked his sippy cup off the kitchen table. Again.

"Careful, buddy," Robert said, picking it up and setting it in front of his son. Robert tried to feel relieved that his already-well-worn copy of *How to Handle the Toddler Years*, which he jokingly called "the owner's manual," assured him that it was perfectly normal for toddlers to knock over cups, throw food, and demonstrate an often-overwhelming amount of emotional instability. But just because it was normal didn't mean it was easy.

"Play phone?" Tyler said, eyeing Robert's phone on the table.

Robert set a bowl of cereal and bananas in front of Tyler. "It's not time for you to play with Daddy's phone. It's time for you to eat your breakfast and get ready for day care."

Tyler, distracted by his bowl of Cheerios, sliced banana, and sippy cup of milk, began happily eating.

That's another thing about two-year-olds, Robert thought. *Their emotions can turn on a dime*. When Robert had last taken Tyler to the pediatrician, he had unloaded on her about Tyler's wild mood swings.

The pediatrician had just laughed and said, "Welcome to parenthood." She had then promised him, as she always did, that the task of parenting would get easier as Tyler got older.

But *when* would it get easier? When Tyler was three? When he was old enough to start school? When he was in college?

Robert knew that for him, the hardest thing about parenting was that it was something he had to do alone. He had never planned to be a single parent, but he had no choice now that Anna was gone.

Robert had met Anna his junior year in college. He had never believed in the "finding the one" theory of romance—surely there wasn't just one person in the whole world who was right for you—and yet his and Anna's connection was immediate. They loved the same books and movies, and when they started having more serious conversations, they discovered that they shared deeper values, too. They dated through the rest of college and got engaged right after graduation, agreeing on a one-year engagement to give them some time to get used to being real grown-ups with real jobs before they got married.

Robert settled into a steady but not terribly exciting job with a local lifestyle magazine, and Anna got a position as a first-grade teacher. They got married barefoot on the beach, and both sets of their parents chipped in to help them out with a down payment on a house. Their little bungalow had seen better days, but it still had plenty of charm, especially for young, energetic first-time homeowners who were willing to put some elbow grease into renovating it.

The only downside, as far as Robert was concerned, was the house's location, right next to the town's most notorious geographical feature: the Cliffs. Although these rocky outcroppings possessed a rugged beauty, they also had a grisly history. The highest of them was nicknamed "Jumper's Cliff" by the locals because it was a common site for suicides over the generations.

THE CLIFFS

It seemed that everyone knew of someone who had chosen to end it all at the Cliffs. The jilted high school homecoming queen from Robert's mother's generation, the businessman who lost all his money due to bad investments, the grandmother with a terminal cancer diagnosis. There were stories about the Cliffs that were fact, and stories that were fiction, but true or not, these tales made people look at the geological features with a mixture of fear and awe, especially Jumper's Cliff. Teenagers gathered there and creeped each other out with scary stories. Younger kids whispered that the ghosts of the departed still haunted the place where they had chosen to make that final leap.

Robert had grown up hearing those stories, and the Cliffs creeped him out. Anna insisted that, while the suicides themselves were sad, the Cliffs were just rocks; they didn't really mean anything. Besides, the house's proximity to the Cliffs was why it had been such a steal. Attributing any dark meaning to the Cliffs was nothing short of superstition.

Robert knew she was right. And once they moved into the house, he was so happy with his new wife and his new life that he hardly thought about the Cliffs at all. When he looked back on it, the first year of their marriage was a blissful blur of love and laughter.

In his mind, he could play out scenes from that first year like a montage in a romantic movie: the two of them riding bikes together, cooking dinner together, cuddling in front of the TV with a big bowl of popcorn between them. Sure, one of them would sometimes have a bad day at work or come down with a cold, but these problems were minuscule compared to the happiness they took in each other's company.

Although the first year of their marriage had been great, the happiest time in Robert's life had come when Anna was pregnant with Tyler. They had been married two years when they found out she was pregnant, and they were both over the moon with delight. There was something about the idea that they had created a new human being because of their love—it seemed almost magical. As happy as they had been as a couple, they knew they would be an even happier family.

Throughout Anna's pregnancy, she had glowed like some kind of ancient mother goddess from mythology. Robert had glowed, too, so full of love he didn't know what to do with all of it. He massaged Anna's feet when they were sore after she came home from teaching all day. He went out to fetch her mint chocolate chip ice cream when she said it was the only thing in life that could possibly satisfy her cravings. They were in perfect harmony during her pregnancy, two dedicated gardeners growing their baby together.

But then things went wrong.

Two months before the baby was due, Anna started complaining of swelling in her hands and feet. When she called the nurse at the obstetrician's office, she had said not to worry about it, that swelling was common among pregnant women, especially in the hottest months of the summer. Reassured, Anna had bought bigger shoes and soaked her feet in Epsom salts and otherwise ignored her symptoms. But when she went in for her regular checkup, her blood pressure was so alarmingly high that the doctor insisted that she be admitted to the hospital immediately.

After that, things were a nightmarish blur in Robert's mind: all the IV drugs the doctors gave her in a failed attempt to bring her blood pressure down, the decision to deliver the baby early by Caesarean section in hopes of saving her life, the massive stroke she suffered on the operating table that left Robert a single father. For a long time, he was numb. None of it even felt real.

Since Tyler was born early, he was tiny and unable to breathe on his own without exhausting himself. He had to stay in the hospital for a few weeks until he gained weight and his lungs developed more. In a shocked daze, Robert would visit his new baby in the neonatal intensive care unit. He would scrub his hands and put on a face mask before entering the brightly lit white room lined with plastic incubators in which impossibly tiny babies lay. Robert would stand by his own son's incubator and look at Tyler's small, skinny body, wearing a diaper the size of a fast-food napkin. The parents of other babies in the NICU always looked tired and worried like Robert did, but they arrived in couples, so at least they had each other.

In horror, Robert would look at his son and think, *Kid, I'm all you have in this world.*

It was not a good way to start out in life—motherless and stuck with a father who couldn't eat, sleep, or go a full hour without crying. In his exhausted, grief-stricken state, there were only two facts Robert knew for sure:

1. He was all that Tyler had.
2. He was not enough.

Robert had muddled through the last two years, managing to hold down his job somehow and provide Tyler with food, clothing, and shelter. Robert had withdrawn from his friends because he didn't want their pity and because for a single father of a toddler, grabbing a bite to eat after work with his buddies was not an option. At five o'clock sharp, he had to leave the office to pick up Tyler from day care. After that, it was time to go home and fix his supper. Then came playtime and bath time and—if Robert was lucky and Tyler would actually fall asleep—bedtime. The toddler owner's manual was clear: Without a regular schedule, life with a toddler descended into chaos. Robert had quite enough chaos in his life, so he tried not to deviate from the daily schedule.

Once Tyler was finally asleep, Robert mindlessly surfed through the channels on TV or played *Warriors' Way* on his laptop. Sometimes Bartholomew, the orange cat, sat with him, but most often, he did not. Bartholomew had been Anna's pet before she and Robert had married, and Anna used to refer to him jokingly as "my first husband" because of the way he guarded her jealously and had never warmed up to Robert. Now, with Anna gone, Bartholomew would accept food or the occasional pat from Robert, but he never gave Robert the impression that he was doing anything more than tolerating him because he was the dispenser of cat food.

Was Robert lonely? Yes, painfully so. But he was also too busy and exhausted to do anything about it. After Tyler's bedtime, he allowed himself two or three hours of mindless screen time of one kind or another until he fell into bed himself, knowing that he was going to wake up to a day that was nearly identical to the one before, with the type and duration of Tyler's mood swings being the only wild card.

Right now, though, as Tyler was contentedly picking up Cheerios and stuffing them in his mouth, he was adorable. His hazel eyes—the same shade as Anna's—were framed by long, sooty eyelashes. His curly black hair surrounded his head like a halo, and his mouth was a cherubic rosebud, also like his mom's. In fact, Tyler resembled his mother so much that it made Robert's heart hurt. Looking at his son, Robert felt overwhelmed by love but also by fear. What if he lost Tyler like he'd lost Anna? Over and over, the what-ifs played on the screen of his mind like a trailer for a movie no one would ever want to see.

Even though Robert couldn't look at Tyler without thinking of Anna, he never talked to Tyler about her. Tyler was too young to understand death, and Robert wasn't doing such a great job of understanding it himself. In his heart, he knew it would probably be a good idea to start showing Tyler pictures of his mom and telling him little stories about the kind of person she was, the things she used to say and do, how excited she had been about becoming his mommy. But he could never bring himself to take out any of the pictures of Anna hidden in the attic. If he tried to talk about her, the words stuck in his throat and he said nothing. Even saying her name hurt too much, especially because when he looked at Tyler, he was staring into Anna's eyes.

Like he did every weekday morning, Robert choked back his sadness along with some black coffee and drove Tyler to day care, letting him play with his phone all the way. After he had dropped off Tyler, he went to work, only nodding at colleagues who greeted him with "good morning." He didn't want to seem rude, but he didn't want to get into a conversation, either. His own reactions were too unpredictable. Once he started talking, what would he say? Would he get all emotional in front of someone he didn't even know very well? Would he break down entirely? And if he did break down, what if he wasn't able to put the pieces back together?

Robert knew that no matter how bad he felt, he had to hold on to his job. It was the only way he could make any kind of life for Tyler. And so today, like every other day, he sat at his cubicle and worked without stopping, trying to empty his mind of everything but the task in front of him. He stopped at noon and took out a sandwich, eating it so mindlessly that once he finished it, he couldn't even have identified what kind of sandwich it had been. He walked to the bathroom, then to the water cooler. He was refilling his water bottle when a voice behind him said, "Hey."

He jumped as though startled that he wasn't the only person in the building. He turned around to see Jess, the nice, bespectacled copy editor and self-confessed "grammar nerd" who had been hired at the same time he was. She and he used to chat a bit before Anna died. Before he was broken.

"Hey, Jess," he said, moving away to let her have a turn at the water cooler and, he hoped, to go back to his desk without being disturbed further. He turned to walk away.

"Hold up a sec," Jess said.

"Me?" Robert said, even though it was clearly him she was talking to. Reluctantly, he turned around.

"I was just noticing you eating your sad little sandwich at your desk." Jess filled up one of those weird paper cones with water from the cooler. Who had decided that those were adequate drinking vessels? She grinned at him. "Well, maybe it was a delicious sandwich, but it looked sad to me. And I was thinking . . . I know you can't go out after work because you've got a kiddo to fetch, but a lot of us go out for half-price sushi on Wednesdays at lunch. Maybe you could go with us sometime?"

Sushi had been Robert and Anna's favorite food. They had learned to love it in college and had also learned to use chopsticks together, picking up sushi rolls, dunking them in soy sauce, and popping them into each other's mouths. While a lot of couples went out for steaks or seafood or Italian for special occasions, for them it was always sushi.

How could going out for half-price sushi with a bunch of random people from work live up to all those romantic sushi dinners with Anna? The answer was simple: it couldn't.

It would only bring back memories to make him sadder.

Still, Jess was nice for asking him. For taking pity on him.

"Yeah, maybe I'll join you sometime," Robert said, not even trying to sound convincing. "Thanks for inviting me."

"Okay," Jess said, sounding surprisingly disappointed. "Robert?"

"Yeah?" He didn't know where this was going but already knew he didn't like it. Wasn't this a workplace? Shouldn't they be working?

She looked down for a minute like she was collecting her thoughts. "You know," she began, "before things changed so much for you, you and I used to be friends. We used to talk. If you ever want to talk again, I'm here."

Robert knew he was in danger of his emotions bubbling up to the surface, which couldn't happen. He couldn't be a basket case at work. He had to get out of this conversation and get back to his desk. "That's very kind—"

Jess rolled her eyes. "I'm not being 'kind,' you goof! I like you. I've always enjoyed your company. And I'm a single parent, too. Not for the same reason you are, maybe, but I bet we still go through a lot of the same stuff. Talking about some of it might be good for our sanity. What's left of it."

Robert felt himself smile a little. Against his will, he was remembering why he had liked Jess. "I'm down to crumbs myself," he said. It was a joke, but like a lot of jokes, it contained the truth.

"I hear you. And who knows? Maybe our kids could hang out. We could take turns watching each other's rug rats so we could maybe have an evening out every once in a while."

"Don't make any promises. You haven't met my kid

yet," Robert said. Had he just made two jokes in a row?

"He's two, right?"

"Yes."

"Well, maybe I should give it a year or two before I offer my babysitting services." She smiled at him, a warm, genuine smile. "Listen, I'm giving you a free pass this week, but next Wednesday, you're going out for half-price sushi with us. No more sad little sandwiches for you."

Robert gave her a little wave. "I will consider your invitation. Thank you." He turned to go back to his cubicle.

"It's not an invitation!" Jess called behind him. "It's mandatory! Mandatory sushi! Which would be a great name for a band, by the way!"

Robert sat back down at his cubicle. He was pretty sure that his conversation with Jess was the longest conversation he had had with a nonfamily member in months. Like someone who hasn't exercised in years and suddenly finds himself back on the treadmill, he was exhausted. No more chitchat today. He stayed at his desk, where he worked nonstop until five. When it was time to leave, he felt no sense of relief. He was simply moving from one series of tasks in one location to another series of tasks in another. Off went the graphic designer hat, on went the dad hat.

Robert pulled into the parking lot of Tiny Tot

Academy and went into the cheerful, red-roofed building to fetch his son. He entered the room with the big red number two on the door. The walls were peppered with construction paper cutouts and unintentionally abstract crayon-scribble drawings. Robert found Tyler's bubbly young teacher, Miss Lauren, surrounded by toddlers playing with the brightly colored toys that cluttered the floor. While being outnumbered by volatile little people seemed terrifying to Robert, Miss Lauren looked perfectly at home and greeted Robert with a smile. She stood up to get closer to Robert's eye level. "He was a happy boy for most of today," she said, "though there is one little thing I should tell you about."

Robert braced himself for bad news. He hoped Tyler hadn't hit some other kid. Or bitten somebody. It seemed like every day care had one kid who was the biter. Nobody wanted to be the biter's parent.

Miss Lauren smiled again. "Don't worry. He didn't attack anybody or anything."

Robert let himself breathe a little.

Miss Lauren pushed back her curly brown hair behind her ears. "It was just that today I asked the kids to draw pictures of their families and talk about them. Being two, most of them just drew blobs or scribbles, but then we sat in a circle and everybody talked about their families and who was in their pictures. Tyler's friend Noah noticed Tyler didn't have a mom in his picture and asked him about it. Tyler got a little upset, I think mostly because someone pointed out his family was different."

Robert hated to think of Tyler being singled out because of his loss. Did that kind of behavior have to start so early?

"Aren't these kids a little young to even notice that kind of thing?" he asked. He looked around at the toddlers in the room, playing with blocks or trucks or dolls. They were babies, really.

Miss Lauren smiled again. "Oh, you'd be surprised what they notice. They don't miss much, believe me. I told Noah and the rest of the class that not all kids have a mommy and a daddy, that there are all different kinds of families, and I talked about what some of those families might look like. I said the only thing you need to have to make a family is people and love. So I guess you could say it turned into a teachable moment."

Robert stiffened. He hated the thought of his and Tyler's broken little family being used as a "teachable moment," and for what? So the other kids could feel sorry for Tyler instead of just making fun of him? He didn't want his son to be the object of ridicule, but he didn't want him to be an object of pity, either.

But there was no point in saying anything negative to Miss Lauren. She was so young and bright-eyed and idealistic that criticizing her would be like kicking a friendly puppy. He finally heard himself say, "Thank you for letting me know." It sounded stiffer and more formal than necessary, but at least it was polite.

"You're welcome," Miss Lauren said. "I just thought I should say something in case, you know, you wanted to talk about it with Tyler at home."

"Right," Robert said. He didn't want to talk about it, not at home with his son and definitely not here with a near stranger. "You ready to go, buddy?" he called to Tyler from across the brightly decorated room.

Tyler looked up from the plastic dump truck he was rolling back and forth and said, "Daddy!" He grinned, jumped up, and ran to Robert, his arms outstretched.

"See?" Miss Lauren said. "A happy boy."

Robert had a hard time taking comfort in this statement. If Tyler was a happy boy, it was only because he didn't yet understand what he was missing.

Robert didn't really want to stop for groceries on the way home, but he didn't see any way around it. Robert didn't care much about eating, but he knew that if nothing else, he had to make sure his kid's basic needs were met. Once he got Tyler safely strapped into his car seat, he said, "We need to stop at the store on the way home, buddy. We're out of milk and juice." Toddlers ran on milk and juice the way cars ran on gasoline. They had to have it, and they burned their way through it at an alarming and expensive rate.

"Milk! Doos!" Tyler said.

"That's right. We'll buy some at the store. You can pick what kind of juice you want."

"Bapple!" Tyler sang. For some reason, when he said the word *apple*, it came out with a *b* at the beginning.

"You want apple juice?" Robert said. This was the way the toddler owner's manual said to handle kids' mispronunciations—not to call attention to them, but to make sure you repeated the word correctly.

"Yeah! Bapple doos!" Tyler cheered.

"You got it, buddy." Robert turned into the All Mart parking lot and prepared himself for the ordeal of shopping.

Tyler owned one T-shirt with Freddy Fazbear on it, but Robert had never thought of his son as a Freddy fanatic. He was too little, for one thing. As he pushed Tyler in the shopping cart past the toy aisles, though, Tyler pointed his index finger and yelled, "Fweddy!" at the top of his tiny lungs.

"What was that, buddy?" Robert asked, looking around to see what Tyler was seeing. For a second he thought Freddy was a kid Tyler recognized from day care.

"Fweddy! Fweddy!" Tyler yelled, his eyes wide with excitement.

Robert followed the line of his son's pointing finger to a display of identical plush brown bears with wide smiles, thick black eyebrows, and black top hats. The packaging proclaimed that what Tyler was looking at was a toy called Tag-Along Freddy. But how did Tyler know that?

With a surge of guilt, Robert realized how Tyler most likely knew. When Robert was especially exhausted or too sad to cope—and this happened more often than he would like to admit—he would plop Tyler down in front of the TV. He only let him watch age-appropriate programming, and the cartoons, while they were no doubt eye candy with bright colors and rapidly shifting images, did at least make a pretense of having some educational value.

But then there were the commercials. The terrible, terrible commercials designed by board rooms of cynical suits on Madison Avenue to make children desire technicolor sugar blobs masquerading as cereal, high-fructose-corn-syrup suspensions masquerading as "juice drinks," and the latest toys based on the most popular of pop culture trends.

"You want to look at one of the Freddys?" Robert asked.

Tyler nodded and held out his hands.

Robert placed the toy in Tyler's hands, and Tyler's mouth spread into a beautiful smile that conjured the ghost of his mother. Even though the bear was encased in cardboard packaging, he drew it to him in a hug. "Wuv," he said.

Well, shoot, Robert thought. It was hard to argue with wuv.

"Now, you be careful with that bear," Robert said. "We haven't decided if we're going to buy it." When he looked at the price sticker, he was surprised how expensive it was. "Yikes," he muttered.

"Buy?" Tyler asked, still clutching the toy to his chest. "Mine?"

"Well, let me read the packaging and see if it's even safe for kids your age," Robert said. He pulled another bear off the shelf and turned it over. The pictures on the back of the box showed laughing toddlers playing with Tag-Along Freddy and, interestingly, a woman dressed like she worked in an office, looking at her wristwatch and smiling like all was well in the world. Robert read the text on the back of the package:

> TAG-ALONG FREDDY IS A KID'S AND A PARENT'S BEST PAL. FREDDY GOES WHERE YOUR LITTLE ONE GOES AND SENDS YOU LIVE UPDATES ON YOUR TAG-ALONG TIME WRISTWATCH (WRISTWATCH INCLUDED) SO YOU'LL KNOW YOUR LITTLE ONE IS HAPPY AND SAFE. YOU MAY HAVE TO BE OUT OF SIGHT SOMETIMES, BUT TAG-ALONG FREDDY IS THE BEAR WHO IS ALWAYS THERE!

Robert thought of all the times he had to tend to something in the kitchen or take an important phone call and leave Tyler unattended. It was amazing what could go wrong in just a few seconds. He recalled once when he left the living room long enough to stir a pot on the stove and returned to find Tyler scaling the bookcase like King Kong climbing the Empire State Building. He could see how this Tag-Along Freddy could come in handy, especially for a single parent like him.

When you took into account that it was a toy that was also a safety device, the price didn't seem too outrageous.

"Tyler," he said, "would you like to take Freddy home with you?"

Tyler's whole face lit up in a beautiful smile. "Yeah, Daddy! Fank you!"

Miss Lauren at day care had told Robert they had been working on pleases and thank-yous, but this was the first time he had ever heard Tyler say, "Thank you," without being prompted by a "What do we say?"

"You're welcome, buddy. And I'm loving those good manners."

Getting the bear and the wristwatch set up and working was mildly annoying but could've been worse. After about fifteen minutes of fussing with directions and batteries, Robert had everything in working order. He handed the bear over to Tyler and said, "Why don't you play with Freddy while I get our supper started?"

"Fweddy!" Tyler said, giving the bear a hug.

In the kitchen, Robert put on a pot of water to boil and dumped the contents of a jar of spaghetti sauce into a pan. He was getting the lettuce, carrots, and cucumbers out of the fridge to start a salad when his Tag-Along

Freddy Time wristwatch vibrated. The screen said, **A message from Freddy**. Robert tapped the screen, and a text appeared:

It's all good. I'm playing with my best buddy!

Cute. Robert couldn't help but smile.

Robert sliced carrots and cucumbers for the salad and put the pasta on to boil. When he went in the living room to tell Tyler it was time to eat, the little boy was holding Freddy on his lap and "reading" to him from one of his little board books, *My First Book of Colors*.

Every time Tyler did something this adorable, Robert wished Anna was here to see it. But who was he kidding? He always wished Anna was here.

"I Fweddy's daddy!" Tyler said.

"You are, huh? That's pretty cool," Robert said. "Are you and Freddy ready for supper?"

Robert expected at least a small argument since Tyler was in the middle of "reading," but he said, "Okay, Daddy," tucked his bear under his arm, and followed Robert to the kitchen.

When he helped Tyler to his place at the table, Tyler set Freddy down in the chair next to him and said, "Fweddy plate!"

"You want Freddy to have a plate, too?" Robert asked.

"Uh-huh," Tyler said, nodding like it was a very serious matter.

Feeling more than a little silly, Robert set a plate and a cup at the spot on the table in front of the toy bear. He set down a plate of spaghetti and a bowl of salad in front of Tyler along with a sippy cup of milk. "Now Freddy has to just eat pretend food, or he'll get all messy," Robert said. "He'll eat pretend spaghetti." And then, because he knew rhymes cracked Tyler up, he said, "Freddy spaghetti!"

Tyler giggled like his dad had just made the funniest joke in the world. "Fweddy sketti!" he yelled, then laughed some more, slapping the table in hilarity.

"He's ready for Freddy spaghetti," Robert said. He was milking the joke, but that's what you did when you had a two-year-old audience. There was not much occasion for subtle wit.

Robert and Tyler ate spaghetti and salad and laughed a lot. Even Robert had to admit it was a fun time.

The downside to feeding a toddler spaghetti was that it made a bath necessary, pronto. Tyler's face was so smeared with orange goo that when he smiled, he looked like a jack-o'-lantern. Somehow he had even managed to get noodles in his hair. "Okay, buddy," Robert said, steeling himself in preparation for a tantrum. "We're going to have to go straight to the bathtub after this."

"Fweddy baff, too?" Tyler asked.

"Freddy can't get wet, but he can come along," Robert said.

"Okay, Daddy," Tyler said, picking up his bear and walking toward the bathroom. Talking Tyler into a bath usually involved such elaborate negotiations Robert felt he should involve the United Nations. He couldn't believe tonight's routine was going so easy.

It was funny, though. As much as Tyler usually argued about bath time, once he was in the water he loved it. Robert threw Tyler's collection of rubber duckies and toy boats in the water, and the boy was happy to splash and play. Robert set Freddy down on Tyler's toddler step stool so he was at a safe distance from the splash zone but Tyler could still see him.

Tyler held up each of his tub toys to "show" to Freddy: "Fweddy, dis my blue boat. Fweddy, dis my yellow ducky."

Two-year-olds loved to show off and brag about their material possessions, Robert had noticed. When Tyler talked to his grandma on the phone, most of what he said was a list of the toys he owned. It was like he was some kind of business tycoon bragging about how many cars and houses he owned.

After Tyler was clean and in his choo-choo train pajamas, Robert tucked him into bed with Tag-Along Freddy.

"You want me to read you a book, buddy?" Robert asked.

"Two books," Tyler said.

Robert pretended to be aghast at such an outrageous request. "Two books?"

"'Cause I'm two," Tyler said, like that explained everything.

"Well, I guess I can't argue with that." Robert scooted a chair next to Tyler's bed and looked over at Tyler's bookshelf.

"The silly chicken," Tyler said.

Robert pulled out the book about the silly chicken.

"Do the voices," Tyler said.

Robert read the book about the silly chicken, complete with silly chicken voices. Tyler giggled because the book was funny but also, Robert suspected, because it was hilarious to hear your parent making a fool of himself.

"Now the piggy one," Tyler said.

Robert obeyed.

By the end of the piggy story, Tyler's eyes were drooping. Seconds after Robert closed the book, Tyler wrapped his arm around his Tag-Along Freddy and went right to sleep.

Robert couldn't believe how much easier the regular tasks of parenting had become with Tag-Along Freddy. He couldn't believe he almost didn't buy the bear because it had seemed too expensive. It would've been worth it at twice the price.

Robert got a soda and a snack from the fridge and settled in to watch a dumb but fun action movie he'd missed because he never got to go to the theater anymore. He knew he could hire a sitter, but he already felt bad leaving Tyler in day care all day. He wanted to spend all the time he could with him. The little boy had already been deprived of a mom. As a dad, Robert already felt he wasn't adequate or enough; the least he could do was try to be present all he could. Just like in school, even if you weren't great at it, you could generally get by if you put in some effort and showed up. It wasn't a great parenting philosophy, but it was one Robert could work with.

As the movie's opening credits ran, Robert felt a buzz from his Tag-Along Time wristwatch. The watch's screen read **A message from Freddy.** He tapped it, and the text said, **Fast asleep.**

Nice. Robert let himself relax.

The movie was the exact kind of thing Anna would have hated, but Robert enjoyed the brainless entertainment of cars chasing each other and guns blazing. He knew he would've enjoyed the movie more if Anna had been beside him, making snarky comments about the improbability of the situations and the cheesiness of the acting. She had always been very tolerant of him being equally snarky when they watched the romantic comedies she liked.

Even with his ever-present loneliness, it was still one of the most relaxing nights he'd had in a long time. He knew he had Tag-Along Freddy to thank for his easy evening.

★ ★ ★

Tag-Along Freddy accompanied Tyler to the breakfast table the next morning and then went with him to day care. Tyler didn't even ask to play with Robert's phone in the car. He cuddled Freddy and talked to him instead.

When they arrived in the classroom, Miss Lauren squatted on the floor to examine Tyler's new toy. "Who's your friend?" she asked.

"Fweddy!" Tyler said, sounding proud and delighted. He held the bear to Miss Lauren's face so it seemed to kiss her cheek.

Miss Lauren laughed. "Freddy's very friendly!"

"I know you usually discourage bringing toys from home," Robert said, "but we got the bear yesterday, and he absolutely refuses to part with it."

Miss Lauren smiled and looked at Tyler, who was cuddling Freddy against his chest. It would be obvious to anyone how happy the toy made him. "Well, then I think we can make an exception in this case."

Robert knew the teachers at the day care cut Tyler some slack because he didn't have a mom, just a sad but well-meaning dad who often seemed incompetent and overwhelmed. While on one hand he didn't like being looked at with pity, on the other hand he was happy to take all the breaks he could get.

Every once in a while, as Robert worked in his cubicle, his Tag-Along Freddy Time wristwatch would vibrate. He would tap it and read a text from Freddy:

Messy fun with finger paints!
Yum! Lunchtime!
Nap time! He's snoozing away!

There was something comforting about those messages, about the way they let Robert picture what Tyler was doing over the course of his day. It made him feel less isolated, like he was part of something. A family. He and Tyler may not have been the complete family that Robert had longed for, but they were still a family.

Just like Miss Lauren had explained the idea of family to Tyler's class, they were people who loved each other. And that had to count for something.

Saturday morning after breakfast, Robert grabbed a second cup of coffee and helped Tyler down from his booster seat. "It's a beautiful morning, buddy! Why don't we go outside and you can play in your sandbox?"

"Yeah! Sandbox!" Tyler said. He grabbed his Freddy doll with one hand and his daddy's hand with the other. "Fweddy play, too."

"Okay," Robert said. "Freddy can come, too. But he can't get in the sandbox. The sand would be bad for his fur."

Robert had settled into some kind of deal with the helpful inanimate object that was Tag-Along Freddy. Freddy would give Robert regular updates on Tyler's safety and well-being, and in return Robert would prevent Tyler from submerging Freddy in water, smearing him with spaghetti sauce, coating him in sand, or exposing him to any other messy form of peril. It was a mutually beneficial relationship.

Outside, Tyler perched Tag-Along Freddy on the side of the sandbox. Robert supposed it was so that Freddy could "watch" him play. Robert settled on a chair on the porch with his cup of coffee and watched Tyler play, too.

Tyler loved his sandbox. It was filled with toy dump trucks and bulldozers and other construction vehicles. Tyler loved taking his plastic shovel, filling his dump truck with sand, moving it around while making *vroom* sounds, and then dumping out the sand, only to fill it up again. It never got old, as far as Robert could tell.

From inside the house, Robert heard his phone ringing. He had meant to bring it outside but had left it on the kitchen counter. Parenting made him so scattered that it seemed he was always leaving something behind.

"Hey, buddy, I'm gonna go get the phone," Robert said. "You stay in the sandbox, okay?"

"Okay, Daddy," Tyler said, shoveling sand into the bed of his dump truck.

"I'll be right back," Robert called.

Robert ran into the kitchen and picked up his phone. The voicemail icon popped up, and he clicked on it. It was a recorded message from a sketchy-sounding company trying to sell him homeowner's insurance he didn't need. He deleted the message and headed back outside.

The sandbox was empty.

Fear gripped Robert's heart. "Tyler!" he yelled. "Tyler!"

No answer.

He ran up to the sandbox. He could see the indentation in the sand where Tyler had been sitting, but no Tyler. Tyler's Tag-Along Freddy still sat on the edge of the sandbox. Clearly Freddy had not been "watching."

Robert looked at the open gate—*it had been closed before, hadn't it?*—and saw a white van he didn't recognize driving away. Could Tyler be inside that van? It was the absolute worst thing he could imagine.

Robert felt his Tag-Along Freddy Time wristwatch vibrate. The watch's screen announced, **A message from Freddy**. He tapped the icon. A one-word message appeared on the screen: **Gone.**

"Gone?" Robert screamed. "Gone? How is that supposed to help me?" He kicked the stuffed bear as hard as he could, sending it sailing across the yard.

"Tyler! Tyler!" he yelled some more. He ran out into the street, yelling. Neighbors came out of their houses to ask what was wrong, but no one had seen his son.

Could someone have opened the gate, come into the yard, and snatched his son in the few seconds it took him to go inside the house and grab his phone? It seemed impossible, and yet you saw that kind of thing on the news all the time. Those people had probably thought it was impossible, too—the kind of thing that happened to other people, but not to you.

Until it did.

His phone. He had forgotten he was still holding his phone. Time was wasting. He called the police.

They arrived quickly, he'd give them that. There were two officers, an older man with salt-and-pepper hair and a young, dark-haired woman.

"So at what time did you notice your son was missing?" the younger officer asked. Her demeanor was professional, but Robert could still hear genuine concern in her voice. Her badge read RAMIREZ.

"Maybe twenty minutes ago?" Robert said. He was so panicky he couldn't get his breath. "He was in the sandbox, I ran into the house to get my phone, and when I came back, he was gone."

"And there's no chance he could've come into the house while you were getting your phone and then hidden somewhere? Some kids get a kick out of hiding," the older officer, whose badge read COOK, said. "You'd be amazed how many kids I've found hiding under beds or in closets, giggling like crazy about how bad they've scared their mom and dad."

"No, I would've heard him if he had come back in the house," Robert said. "Also, the front gate was open when I came back—I'm pretty sure it was closed before. And I saw a white van on the street. I know it doesn't belong to anybody in the neighborhood. Maybe he was abducted by someone in that van."

Officer Ramirez was taking notes furiously. "Did you get the van's license plate number?"

"No. It drove away too fast. I'm sorry." In fact, Robert hadn't even thought of trying to get the van's license plate number. *You would think I'd never even seen a cop show on TV,* he thought. *I'm incompetent. I'm too incompetent to be a parent, and now Tyler is paying the price.*

"That's okay," Officer Ramirez said. "I know this is upsetting. I just need to go through all of these questions so we'll have the information we need to find your son. Now . . . does your son's mother live with you?"

"No. She died in childbirth having Tyler."

If she weren't dead, Robert thought, *Tyler probably wouldn't be missing because he at least would have had one competent parent.*

"I'm sorry to hear that," Officer Ramirez said. "Could you give us a physical description of your son?"

"He's two years old," Robert said. "Hazel eyes. Dark hair. He's about three feet tall, and I think he weighed twenty-eight pounds on his last doctor's visit." Conjuring up a vivid picture of Tyler made his disappearance all the more painful. Three feet tall and twenty-eight pounds—he was so tiny, so helpless. "H-here—I can send you a picture of him." He fumbled with his phone.

"Can you tell us what clothing Tyler was wearing at the time of his disappearance?" Officer Ramirez continued.

What clothes had Robert picked out for Tyler this morning? He hadn't paid much attention because he wasn't anticipating being quizzed on them. "Play clothes. Blue shorts, I think, and a T-shirt with Freddy Fazbear on it." Saying the bear's name made him think painfully of the message on his wristwatch: *Gone*.

He had to pull himself together. For Tyler's sake. "Red sneakers," he said. "And he's still in diapers if that matters." Tears sprang to his eyes. Tyler was still just a baby.

"Thank you," Officer Ramirez said.

"So . . . what are you going to do to find him?" Robert asked.

Officer Cook, who had seemed content to let his partner ask most of the questions, finally chimed in. "Sir, when a child this young is missing, you can be sure it's not something we take lightly. We'll scour the entire area. We'll see if we can get any info about that van. And we'll be in touch. Right now home is the best place for you to be, with your phone close by."

"Are you going to put out one of those alerts for missing children?" Robert asked. He couldn't remember what the alerts were called, but he got them on his phone with some frequency and always found them upsetting. He couldn't help imagining the frightened children, the frantic parents. Now he was one of those parents.

"An Amber Alert?" the older officer said. "We will if we don't find him quickly and if we feel like he's in any immediate danger."

"Of course he's in danger!" Robert shouted. "He's two years old, and he's either run off by himself or has been abducted by a maniac. How could he not be in danger?"

"We understand you're upset," Officer Ramirez said, patting his arm. "This is every parent's worst nightmare. But we're going to do everything in our power to get Tyler back to you as quickly as possible, safe and sound."

It was 5:00 p.m., and there were still no leads. The police had assured him that they were asking around about the suspicious white van but hadn't received any useful information yet.

Robert sat on the couch, staring ahead in a daze. He had never felt so useless, so worthless. He only had one job that mattered, and that was to keep his son safe. He had failed miserably. Everyone he loved died or disappeared. He couldn't protect anyone, and now he was all alone. It probably served him right.

Robert's wristwatch vibrated. He felt a sudden small flutter of hope. Maybe the watch had some information about Tyler's whereabouts. He tapped **A message from Freddy.** A text appeared: **Why don't you go to the Cliffs?**

Robert shivered as though the temperature in the room had dropped by forty degrees. Jumper's Cliff. His own thoughts had been headed in that direction—without Anna, without Tyler, what reason did he have to keep on living? Apparently he was so worthless that even a child's toy thought he was a waste of good organs.

Stop, Robert thought. Tyler hadn't even been missing for eight full hours. If he was still alive, Robert had to be there for him. He wasn't much, but he was all Tyler had. He would try to do better, try not to fail his son the next time.

He looked over at the mantel where he had set the Tag-Along Freddy when he brought it back into the house. He knew it was ridiculous, but he felt like the bear was mocking him. Judging him. Robert wasn't a superstitious person, but he couldn't shake the feeling that the toy was somehow bad luck. He grabbed it, holding it between his thumb and forefinger as if it were a dead rat. He carried it outside, lifted the lid on the garbage can, and dumped it inside.

Back in the house, Robert sat back down on the couch. Normally at this time, he'd be thinking about what he and Tyler could have for supper. Usually on Saturdays, he made something simple—hot dogs or grilled cheese sandwiches. Sometimes he'd order a pizza and they'd watch one of the movies Tyler loved, the kind with cartoon animals being heroic.

Robert wished he could be heroic.

His phone rang. He answered before it had time to ring twice.

"Mr. Stanton? This is Detective Ramirez."

"Did you find him?" Robert's heart was pounding in his chest.

"Not yet, sir, but we have officers out all over the city. We also have use of a dog that has a tremendous track record when it comes to locating missing persons. I know this seems like an irregular request, but do you have some piece of clothing that belongs to your son that we could give to the dog to sniff? An unwashed shirt of his that's in the laundry hamper, maybe?"

"I'm sure I do, yes." Robert was always behind on laundry. He counted it as one of his many failings, but in this case, maybe it could actually be helpful.

"Well, if it's okay with you, I may come by and get it."

"Yes, of course," Robert said, trying to keep his voice from breaking. "Anything that might help you find him."

Once he was off the phone, Robert went into Tyler's room. He looked at Tyler's little toddler bed and thought about all the nights he had peeked into the room and seen Tyler there, sleeping in that deep, peaceful way that only small children can sleep. He would give anything to see Tyler lying there right now. Anything.

He reached into the laundry hamper and pulled out the blue-and-white-striped shirt Tyler had worn just the day before. When he held it up, it seemed impossibly small, like doll clothes. He held the shirt to his nose and inhaled. Playground dirt; apple juice; a sweet, hay-like aroma he thought of as little-boy smell. His little boy's smell.

Robert sat down on Tyler's bed, put his face in his hands, and sobbed.

By the time Detective Ramirez arrived to pick up the shirt, Robert had calmed down a little, but his eyes were still red and swollen.

"I know this is hard," Detective Ramirez said. "Probably the hardest thing you've ever been through. But I promise you we will do all that we can to find your little boy. Try to get some rest, okay?"

After the officer left, Robert sank back onto the living room couch. This was probably the hardest thing he had ever been through, but losing Anna had been terribly hard, too. He knew everybody had some bad things happen to them, but he certainly felt like he had had more than his fair share of suffering.

His phone vibrated. He clicked on the message icon. The text read, **Why don't you go to the Cliffs?**

Robert's anger flashed white-hot. Maybe it wasn't so crazy to think the bear was judging him. After all, it was urging him to commit suicide. Well, he wasn't going to have it. He stomped outside to the garbage can where he had dumped the thing.

He brought the bear back into the house. Somehow it made him less nervous to have the thing where he could see it.

He hoped he wasn't losing his mind. He was under an unthinkable amount of stress, of course, but he needed to keep it together for Tyler.

Rest. Detective Ramirez told him to get some rest. Instead of going back to the couch, Robert walked down the hallway to his bedroom, carrying the bear.

He set the bear down on the bed. Looking at it, he felt such a surge of hate for the toy that his stomach roiled. He ran to the bathroom and retched into the toilet, though not much came up. He hadn't eaten since breakfast.

Breakfast seemed like years ago. Everything had still been normal at breakfast.

Everything had been normal until he had brought Tag-Along Freddy into the house.

Back in the bedroom, Robert glared at the offending bear. He drew back his fist and punched it in the face again and again. It quickly became apparent that the punches weren't at all effective. The bear's face would cave in when Robert's fist made contact with it, but then it sprung right back into place. Robert wasn't doing it any harm, and the one thing he wanted, other than getting Tyler back home safely, was to harm the bear.

Robert grabbed Tag-Along Freddy by its ear and carried it downstairs. He went into the kitchen and retrieved the box of matches he kept on a high shelf in a cabinet out of Tyler's reach. He carried Freddy outside to the trash can and threw him back in. He struck a match and held it to the bear, waiting for it to catch fire.

The bear's foot smoldered a little but refused to burst into flames. It was probably treated with some chemical, Robert thought, to make it flame-retardant. A safety feature. Well, he'd put a stop to that. He grabbed the bottle of lighter fluid he kept near the grill.

Robert doused the bear with lighter fluid. Then he struck another match and threw it into the garbage can. Tag-Along Freddy went up in a satisfying *whoosh* of flames. Robert watched it burn for a few minutes, then used his garden hose to extinguish the fire. He didn't want to accidentally burn the whole house down.

Once the fire died out, he felt a small amount of relief. He knew it didn't make any logical sense, but he still felt as if destroying the bear would somehow help find Tyler.

At the very least there wouldn't be a voice that kept telling Robert to kill himself.

Now he could rest, just like Officer Ramirez had ordered him to. After he made sure the last of the fire was extinguished, he went back to his bedroom, undressed, and crawled under the covers. He was pretty sure there was no way he was going to sleep, but it was still a relief to lie down. He was so exhausted that every bone and muscle in his body felt heavy as lead. He didn't lose consciousness but lay there in a sort of stupor, his eyes open but not really seeing.

The vibration of the Tag-Along Time wristwatch startled Robert.

But that was impossible. He had destroyed the bear. It couldn't send him messages anymore. Maybe he really was asleep and this was a dream. Wouldn't it be wonderful if all of this had just been a really bad dream?

Robert slapped his own face and felt the sting. He wasn't dreaming.

He lifted his arm and looked at the watch. **A message from Freddy** was flashing. With a shaking hand, he tapped the icon. **Why don't you go to the Cliffs?**

"No!" Robert yelled, clapping his hands over his ears. "No! This is impossible! The bear is practically just ashes now! It can't still be telling me to kill myself. It can't be telling me anything!"

Robert ran outside and lifted the lid of the garbage can. The Freddy doll was charred, but it was still grinning. He reached inside the can and pulled it out. The bear stank of smoke and lighter fluid and was singed and blackened in some places, but it was still intact.

Robert knew that he spent too much time without adult company since Anna died, and sometimes he felt so sad and lonely that he wondered if he should see a therapist. But now, it seemed, he had moved beyond the need to just talk to a caring professional. The trauma of losing Tyler after losing Anna had caused him to lose something else: his mind.

But he had destroyed the bear. He knew what he had seen.

When Robert had first seen the bear in the store, he thought it was cute—a nice, cuddly friend for his little boy. But now the bear's once-charming smile looked malevolent. Its black eyebrows seemed to slant downward in a classic cartoon depiction of evil. It was all clear now: Robert had brought the bear into the house, and Tyler had disappeared. Tyler's disappearance was the bear's fault.

The bear could not continue to exist.

Robert fished his car keys out of his pocket. He placed the bear in the driveway in the direct path of his car's left front tire, and then got into the car and started it. He felt only slight resistance as he drove over the bear, then put the car in reverse and backed over it. He then ran over it one last time, leaving the bear's body trapped beneath the tire, a furry Freddy pancake.

Going back inside the house, he heard his phone ringing. How could he be so stupid as to leave his phone inside? This was the exact kind of stupidity that got Tyler kidnapped in the first place. He ran to answer it. "Yes?" he panted, out of breath.

"Mr. Stanton, this is Detective Ramirez. Are you okay?"

It was such an absurd question that he almost laughed. Of course he wasn't okay. His child was missing, and he had just spent the past five minutes intentionally running over that child's favorite stuffed toy. These were not the actions of a person who was okay. He decided her question didn't deserve an answer. Instead, he asked the only question that mattered, "Did you find him?"

"Not yet, Mr. Stanton, but I wanted to let you know that the dog has his scent now and is searching for him. We also have the tag numbers of every white van in the metro area, and we're running them to see if any of the owners have a history of criminal activity. We're working hard to find your boy. I'll call you in the morning and update you."

Morning seemed like years away. How was he going to make it until morning without Tyler, without even any information about Tyler? "Is there anything I should be doing?"

"Stay close to the phone. Get some rest. Pray, if you're the praying sort. And stay hopeful."

"Thank you," Robert said. But really, other than destroying the bear, there was nothing he could do. He was a helpless, hopeless case.

Just as he hung up the phone, his wristwatch vibrated.

"How?" he yelled. "How?"

He knew what it was going to say, and he was sorely tempted to run it over just like the bear, but there was still a tiny chance—wasn't there?—that the watch might have some connection to Tyler, that it might help locate him some way. He gritted his teeth and tapped **A message from Freddy.**

Why don't you go to the Cliffs?

Broken, Robert sank to his knees and cried.

The more the bear told him to go to the Cliffs, the more suicide seemed like a welcome relief from his pain. Sure, it would be terrifying, standing on the edge, looking down at the jagged rocks below, and willing himself to jump. But the fall would be so fast he wouldn't have time to think or feel anything, and the force with which he'd smash into the rocks would be so hard he would die instantly. Even if there was some physical pain, it would still hurt less than the emotional pain that was ripping him apart. Without Anna and Tyler, what reason did he have to live?

If he went to the Cliffs, he could join Anna in death. Maybe there was even a possibility he would see her again on some other spiritual plane. And of course, it was possible that Tyler was also—

This thought was so horrifying that it sent Robert running back to the bathroom to retch up the nonexistent contents of his stomach. He leaned over the toilet, gagging and sobbing. *My little boy, my little boy* were the words that played in a loop in his head. He flushed the toilet and stood up straight. He caught a glance of himself in the mirror and was shocked by what he saw.

He seemed to have aged ten years in a single day. His complexion was gray, and his eyes were swollen and bloodshot. His face was streaked with tears and snot. On impulse, he turned on the water in the shower. Maybe standing under the spray would calm him down a little, loosen the painful knots in his shoulders. He undressed and stepped into the stall. Letting the hot jets of water pound his neck and shoulders, he felt his exhausted mind begin to wander.

Tyler's first birthday. Knowing the joy that one-year-olds take in destruction, Robert had gotten Tyler a special "smash cake" he could destroy in addition to a larger birthday cake that Robert could slice and serve. Tyler sat in his high chair, wearing a conical paper birthday hat. When the smash cake was set before him, he cackled with delight and immediately jammed both fists into it. He brought his fists down into the cake again and again, then eventually gave one of his frosting-covered hands an experimental lick. Apparently liking what he had discovered, he dove into the cake face-first, coming up with a mouth and a face full of frosting.

Robert had filmed the whole thing, laughing.

Robert had been so happy that day. He had thought about how that day was the first of many happy birthdays for his son, the first of many birthdays he and Tyler would celebrate together.

He had been wrong.

Freddy's words echoed in his head. *Why don't you go to the Cliffs?*

Two years before the birthday party. Robert and Anna's first anniversary. The official gift for the first wedding anniversary was supposed to be paper. Robert had checked out a book on origami from the library, and after a lot of failures and frustration, had learned how to make origami cranes. For weeks, he spent every spare minute he had folding pieces of paper into cranes. The night of their anniversary, they had gone to their favorite sushi restaurant, and Robert had presented Anna with a box of one hundred origami cranes, one crane, he said, for every year of happiness they would have together.

Robert had known realistically that he and Anna couldn't possibly have one hundred years together. But in his darkest nightmares, he never would have dreamed that they had only one year left. Were some people just doomed to lose everyone they loved? Or was it just Robert's own personal curse?

Those words again: *Why don't you go to the Cliffs?*

Robert stood under the shower until the water ran cold and he started to shiver. He turned off the faucet and grabbed a towel. He dried himself off and put on his bathrobe, but he was still shaking, not just with cold but with sadness and fear.

How could the bear still be threatening him? Hadn't he destroyed it? Robert remembered the line from the description on the toy's packaging: *Tag-Along Freddy is the bear who is always there.*

Robert threw on an old T-shirt and a pair of shorts, then grabbed scissors from the bathroom cabinet. He ran out of the house and into the driveway. He yanked the doll out from under his car tire, laid it flat on its back on the hood of the car, and stabbed it over and over and over where its heart would be. If it had a heart.

"What do I have to do to make you go away?" Robert yelled as he kept on stabbing the little bear. "Why won't you just die? You're not even supposed to be alive!" The bear's chest was slashed to ribbons. Bits of stuffing poked out from between the tears.

Robert was debating ripping out the stuffing when his wristwatch vibrated. He knew what to expect. He knew it would be awful. But the little flutter of hope from somewhere inside him whispered, "What if . . . ? What if it's news about Tyler? What if I can save him?"

He took a deep breath and tapped **A message from Freddy**.

Why don't you go to the Cliffs?
Why don't you go to the Cliffs?
Why don't you go to the Cliffs?

"Why don't—"

Robert ripped off the watch and threw it against the pavement, smashing it. Finally, the watch was silent.

He picked up the bear and looked in its blank, googly eyes. All of his rage, all of his pain had turned into a numbness that was somehow even worse. "Fine," he said to the bear, feeling more emotionally drained than he had ever felt. "We'll go to the Cliffs together."

It's the only logical thing to do, Robert thought.

Robert was empty. He was a shell, like a house that had burned so that all of its insides were destroyed. It might not look so bad from the outside, but really, there was nothing left to save. It was time to bring in the wrecking ball. The final demolition was just a formality.

He picked up the bear and went into the house. In the kitchen, he filled the cat's food bowl until it was overflowing and put out an extra bowl of water. That should hold Bartholomew until the police discovered Robert's body and came to search the house.

The police could turn the cat over to the animal shelter, and the shelter could find it a new home. It had never liked Robert anyway.

Robert toyed briefly with the idea of leaving a note, but who would read it? Who would care? If he had anybody left to write a note to, he wouldn't be going to the Cliffs in the first place. He grabbed the bear and walked out the front door, leaving it unlocked to make things easier for the police when they arrived to investigate.

With Tag-Along Freddy in hand, he walked toward the Cliffs. The night sky was changing from black to an early morning gray. A neighbor whose name Robert couldn't remember was already up for his morning run. He slowed down when he saw Robert and started jogging in place. "Any news about your son?" the man asked. The neighborhood gossip machine was apparently working as effectively as usual.

Robert couldn't bring himself to speak, so he just shook his head no.

"I'm sure he's fine," the man said, which Robert knew was a lie. How could this man be so sure when the police didn't even have any information? "Let me know if you need anything."

Robert knew the man meant well, but really, "Let me know if you need anything" was an absurd thing to say to someone in Robert's situation. *I need my son back*, Robert thought. *But since the universe is too cruel to let me have that, I need to jump off the Cliffs. If you can't help me with either of these things, then you are of no use to me. Good-bye.*

The man continued his run, and Robert started running in the opposite direction. But Robert wasn't moving like a man getting some exercise. He was running like a man pursued by demons.

He ran until he reached the Cliffs. He made a beeline for the one everybody called Jumper's Cliff, still holding his small stuffed enemy. When he stood at the summit and looked down at the rocky ground far below, it felt like his stomach dropped into his shoes. He had always been afraid of heights but had always considered it a sensible fear. It wasn't crazy to be afraid of something that could actually kill you. And now, even though death was his goal, he still felt afraid when he looked down.

Robert held up the teddy bear and stared at it. "This is what you want, right?" he asked.

Tears clouded Robert's eyes as he thought of Anna dying on the operating table during what should have been the happiest occasion of their life, the birth of their son. She never would have chosen to make such an early exit from life. She wouldn't have wanted Robert to make an early exit, either, especially when, unlike her, he had a choice.

The living Robert had been doing since Anna died wasn't really living. Anna wouldn't have wanted that for him, either. She wouldn't have wanted him to shut out his friends and eat sad little sandwiches at his desk at work. She would've wanted him to go out with his coworkers and eat half-price sushi. She would've wanted him to enjoy fatherhood but also enjoy the company of other grown-ups. Anna had loved life and had loved Robert. She wouldn't have wanted him to give up on himself.

And she wouldn't have wanted him to give up on Tyler, either, not when there was even a small hope that he might be alive.

He thought of Tyler when he would stretch his arms

up and say, "Pick me up, Daddy," when he would giggle and say, "Daddy silly!" or when they would play Tickle Monster or the rhyming game or read books together. It was easy to get overwhelmed by the daily stresses of parenting—the effort of keeping a child clean and fed and cared for day in and day out. And it was undeniable the will of a toddler often posed a formidable challenge. But the truth was that most of the time he and Tyler spent together was great. He wouldn't trade it for anything.

If there was just one small chance he could hear his little boy's voice again . . .

Robert held up the despised bear and stared into its empty eyes. He drew back his arm and pitched the doll as hard as he could over the edge of the cliff. He spat over the ledge in defiance of what the evil toy had almost made him do. Of what he had almost let the toy make him do.

"Tyler wouldn't want me to!" Robert screamed after the bear plummeted to the rocks below. His voice echoed—"to to to"—in the canyon.

Robert looked down at the rocks below but also up at the sky, where the dawn had turned the clouds a rosy pink, the color of a dress Anna used to wear. He always told her that dress brought out the roses in her cheeks.

*Anna had wanted to live. Tyler—please let him still be alive—*Robert thought—*wanted to live.* The two of them would want Robert to live, too.

Robert looked down at the rocky ground beneath

him and then up at the pink clouds above him. Life was hard, but it could also be beautiful. The two people he loved most in the world wouldn't want him to lose sight of that.

As the sun rose, Robert heard the early morning chirping of birds and the cry of some small animal he couldn't identify. The mewling of a kitten, perhaps? The cries were coming from below him in one of the many holes that had created shallow miniature caverns in the rock face.

The more Robert listened to the cries, he decided they sounded almost human. Could it be—?

Robert's heart felt as though it might pound right out of his chest. He made his way to the underside of the cliff. He had to resist the dangerous temptation to run. How embarrassing that would be—if he had decided to live and then fell off the cliff by accident? As he got closer to the caverns, the cries became more distinct, a high keening that could be a wounded animal but also could be a frightened human child.

Robert stood in front of the openings in the rock face, hoping that he would see his son and not a wounded animal that might attack him out of fear. "Tyler!" he yelled. "Tyler, is that you?"

"Daddy!" Tyler's voice, weak from crying, came from the hole nearest Robert. "Daddy! Daddy, come get me!"

The hole wasn't wide enough for Robert's shoulders

to fit through. "I can't fit in that hole, buddy. You're going to have to come to me. Come toward my voice, buddy! You can do it!"

He could hear scrabbling in the hole, and then, in what couldn't have been more than a minute, Tyler poked his head out of the rocky opening like some kind of woodland creature. He held out his arms, and Robert scooped him up and hugged him. Tyler was dirty and sweaty from his overnight stay in the caverns, but to Robert, he still smelled sweeter than anything else in the world. "You scared me half to death, buddy," Robert said, holding Tyler close. "Why in the world did you run off like that?"

"I saw a doggie," Tyler said like it was the most logical answer in the world.

"So you tried to follow the doggie and got lost?"

"Uh-huh." Tyler rested his head on Robert's shoulder.

"Well, that was really dangerous, buddy. You should never leave the yard unless I'm with you. Promise me you'll never do that again."

"Okay, Daddy," Tyler said. Robert hoped he meant it.

"Good. Let's go home."

"Yeah, carry me," Tyler said, and Robert could hear the tiredness in his voice.

"Okay, buddy." Robert was tired, too, but now that he had found his son, he felt like he had the strength to carry him for a million miles.

As Robert carefully walked away from Jumper's Cliff, Tyler said, "Daddy?"

"Yes, buddy?"

"I'm thirsty."

"I bet you are. We'll get you a big cup of water as soon as we get home."

"And can I have a peanut nana?"

"Sure." Robert knew the kid must be starving. He hadn't eaten since breakfast the day before. Robert was happy to have the opportunity to make Tyler his favorite snack again, sliced bananas with peanut butter to dip them in. Toddlers liked to eat things they could dip into other things. "And I'll make my special mac and cheese for supper, okay?"

"Yummy!"

Honestly, Robert's mac and cheese wasn't anything special, just a mix from a blue box. But it would be special because Tyler was back and unharmed and they'd be eating it together. From now on, all their time together would be special.

A thought occurred to Robert as they reached the lower cliffs. "Hang on just a second, buddy. I want to see something." Without getting too close to the edge, Robert peered down in the direction in which he'd thrown Tag-Along Freddy. The little bear was nowhere to be seen.

"What you see, Daddy?" Tyler asked.

"Nothing, buddy. But look how pretty the sky is.

Your mommy used to have a dress the color of those clouds." He decided he would no longer keep silent about Anna. Tyler needed to hear about his mom, just as Robert needed to talk about her. If they talked about her, if they thought about her, there was a way in which she would still be with them.

"Mommy pretty," Tyler said.

"Yes, she was," Robert said. "Would you like to look at some pictures of your mommy sometime soon?"

"Yeah!" Tyler said.

Tomorrow, Robert decided, he would take the photos of Anna down from the attic. He could put some on the mantel in the living room and maybe one in Tyler's room, too. "We'll do that tomorrow, then," Robert said. "And I can tell you some stories about her, too. Your mommy was very pretty and smart and nice."

"Daddy's nice, too," Tyler said.

It was a high compliment from a two-year-old. "Thanks, buddy. I love you," Robert said, holding Tyler securely as he walked farther and farther away from the Cliffs.

"I love you, Daddy."

"I love you, too, buddy." Robert set Tyler down on the ground. Tyler slipped his hand into his daddy's, and they walked together toward home.

THE BREAKING WHEEL

"I. Hate. Him," Reed whispered through gritted teeth.

From across the aisle of desks, Shelly blew long dark bangs from her forehead, glanced at the back of Julius's head, and then rolled her eyes at Reed. "Tell me something I don't know."

Reed looked at her sideways. "Just sayin'."

Julius, as usual, had been bragging about his talents, and then he'd started complaining. Typical Julius. He was either telling everyone how he was better than they were, or he was trying to blame his problem on someone else. Too often, Reed had been on the receiving end of that blame, along with the physical bullying that came with it.

"You need to ignore him," Shelly said.

"As if," Reed hissed. "He's the world's biggest—"

"Did you have something to add to Julius's observations?" Ms. Billings asked Reed.

Ms. Billings was the perfect teacher for this class: small and compact, a plain face generally devoid of emotion. The head of their robotics class moved in jerky, precise movements that had sparked more than one conversation about whether she was an advanced robot herself.

The first week of class, Shelly's twin brother (and Reed's other best friend), Pickle, had posited, "Who better to teach robotics than AI?" Pickle was convinced Ms. Billings was an android. For weeks, he'd been devising a plan to prove his hypothesis. Because, so far, the plan involved cutting into Ms. Billings, Shelly wouldn't let Pickle go forward with it.

So, what was under the teacher's pale skin was still a mystery.

Reed tipped his chair forward and sat up straight at his desk. In response to Ms. Billing's question, he said, "Um, no?"

Reed couldn't add to Julius's observations because he hadn't heard them. All he heard when Julius talked was the jerk's loud, nasally twang.

Julius never said anything you wanted to hear anyway. He only spoke in insults, complaints, or brags.

Ms. Billings left her cool blue-eyed gaze on Reed long enough for him to start squirming before she shifted her attention back to the class as a whole. She flipped her long, wavy blonde hair off her shoulder as she spoke. "So let's talk about Julius's concern. What could Dilbert do to prevent his remote from affecting Julius's exosuit?"

Reed knew the class discussion was going to be a rehash of IR versus RF remotes, and since it had bored him the first time, he decided not to listen a second time. Besides, it wouldn't matter how much he listened. At this point in the semester, he knew he was going to crash and burn on his project in spite of whatever he learned or didn't learn.

Reed looked at the midsize, partially constructed exoskeleton sitting on his desk. He'd been working on it since Ms. Billings assigned their spring semester project, but it looked like he'd just started because he seemed to have missed too much pertinent information in the class lectures. He'd tried to use the textbook to help him fill in the blanks, but he didn't completely understand it.

When Ms. Billings had first introduced the concept

of exoskeletons, she'd defined them as "crude frames that could be attached to other things for added mobility." She'd then explained how that could be expanded upon if the frames' power sources could add enough functionality to control the wearer. That's what had given him his great project idea. He'd intended to make something to fit over his little sister Alexa's extremely annoying baby doll. He thought it would be cool to make the little doll scare his sister—a classic brotherly prank. But his vision, at this point, wasn't likely to become a reality.

Shelly and Pickle had their projects over halfway done before Reed had gotten even a tenth of the way through his. And now they were both finished, a couple weeks before the project was due.

Admittedly, Pickle's robot was puny, about the size of a small remote-controlled car—just a vaguely man-shaped small metal skeleton with not a lot of personality. Pickle's robot wasn't much to look at, but his robot had mad abilities. With his tricked-out custom remote, he could practically make the thing breakdance. Shelly's robot was similar, but dog-shaped instead of man-shaped. It was about the size of her Labrador, Thales, who was named after some man Shelly said was the first scientist. Living between 624 BC and 545 BC, "Thales of Miletus" was an ancient Greek dude who did a lot of science and mathematics stuff. Reed could remember the guy's name and when he lived, but for some reason he couldn't remember anything Shelly had said the guy did. Not that any of it mattered. What mattered was that Shelly's robot was supposed to mimic a well-behaved dog, and from what Reed could tell, she could probably win a dog show with the thing. She was going to get an A, like she always did.

Why did he let the twins talk him into taking this class anyway? Sure, they were his best friends, but that didn't make him a science nerd like them. Reed was into computers, but not as they related to robotics. He wanted to combine his love for fiction with his aptitude for programming to become a game designer. He wasn't an engineer, and he sucked at building things. Shelly and Pickle knew this. After all, Shelly was the one who couldn't let a year go by without reminding him of his complete ineptitude going all the way back to the building blocks they'd played with when they were five years old. They were freshmen now, and yet Shelly got the giggles at every science model and historical event diorama assigned to them. Every one of Reed's construction efforts reminded her of the "log cabin" five-year-old Reed had built, a cabin that looked less like a cabin and more like the aftermath of an explosion. But in spite of that good-natured ribbing, he knew Shelly hadn't talked him into this class just so she could laugh at him. And as for Pickle, he was too uninterested in others' shortcomings to orchestrate Reed's humiliation.

"It's fun when we take classes together," Shelly had said to Reed when he signed up.

Pickle had grunted what could have been agreement or noncommittal disinterest.

The truth was that Reed would do pretty much anything Shelly wanted him to do. They were friends, and they'd been friends for too long for her to think of him as anything but a friend. But he spent more time than he'd ever admit thinking about what it would be like if he and Shelly were *more* than friends. But after almost ten years, the idea was still what his dad would call a "castle in the sky."

But maybe it wasn't. Sometimes, when he talked to Shelly, she'd look at him with something like admiration, as if she was considering him in a different light.

Take the cliché *castle in the sky*, for instance. One day, when Reed, Pickle, and Shelly were getting off the bus, Shelly was talking about wanting something that was "impossible." Reed had spotted clouds that looked exactly like a castle. He'd pointed at the castle-shaped clouds and said to Shelly, "Look, a castle in the sky. That means impossible dreams can happen, even if it's in another dimension." He was just messing around. But Shelly said, "Actually, you're right." And she'd squinted at him like he'd suddenly gotten interesting.

Reed looked over at Shelly now. Her attention on Ms. Billings, Shelly was chewing on the ends of her thick black hair. She wore it in a meticulous chin-length style, which put the ends right at mouth level. She always chewed on her hair when she was concentrating. It was one of the few little imperfections he noticed about her, and just like all her other imperfections, it was hopelessly charming.

Nah, he didn't think Shelly and Pickle wanted him to humiliate himself for their amusement. That was mean, and they weren't mean. Maybe they were a little thoughtless sometimes, because they'd get wrapped up in their books and their projects and forget to act like normal kids, but they weren't mean.

Now, *Julius*, he was mean.

Reed shot a dirty look at the artful blond waves cascading down the back of Julius's head. Shelly once told Reed that Julius's hair was "dreamy" even though she admitted his personality was somewhere between detestable and execrable. The latter word, among others, taught Reed to never again buy her a word-of-the-day calendar for her birthday.

"Why does he have to use an RF remote?" Julius whined to Ms. Billings. "I don't want his stupid remote to be telling my exoskeleton what to do."

My ears, Reed thought. When Julius whined, his voice climbed an octave, and he sounded like a frightened weasel with a head cold. Who cared about the dreamy hair? *Makes me gag*, Reed thought. And who cared that Julius was tall and muscular, and shallow girls who rated boys on looks and/or money instead of character thought he was a stud? Julius's voice told listeners everything they needed to know about him—he was a sniveling weasel who acted like an ass so people wouldn't notice all that sniveling weasel-ness.

All the expensive clothes Julius wore didn't cover his essential weasel identity, either. No amount of skinny black jeans, gazillion-dollar basketball shoes, designer shirts, or cashmere scarves could disguise a true weasel.

Reed looked at the dangling metal foot of Julius's gangly exoskeleton, which hung off the right side of Julius's desk. Julius's project was a skeletal "suit" he intended to wear. A collection of metal frameworks attached to mechanical "joints" at the shoulders, elbows, hips, and knees, Julius's exosuit had leather straps and metal clamps that would hold the contraption in place on Julius's body. He'd been bragging that it would make him even faster and stronger than he already was. Whatever.

Reed thought exosuits looked a little like scaffolding—what a race of tiny people might create and attach to a human body so they could climb up and repair it. Reed wished Julius's suit was scaffolding and there was a race of tiny people who could fix Julius, who was certainly in need of repair.

"Dilbert?" Ms. Billings said. Pickle looked up—his real name was Dilbert, but his family and close friends called him Pickle, a play on Dill.

"Can you explain to the class your reasoning for using an RF remote?"

"Sure. But I'm not just using an RF remote. I'm using the RF as an IR extender. I want my remote to be effective through walls." Pickle sniffed. "I don't think the problem is my remote anyway. I've achieved my goal with my remote. If he hasn't achieved his goal, isn't it up to him to make adjustments? Why doesn't he"—Pickle pointed at Julius—"install an RFI filter in his signal path? Or he could change his frequency. Or he could check his macros. He may have them programmed too close to mine."

Pickle sniffed again. He didn't have a cold; he was just a perpetual sniffer. Short and dark like his twin sister, Pickle unfortunately didn't get his sister's looks. Shelly was really pretty. It was just that no one, other than Reed, seemed to notice it because she was so intense. Or maybe it had to do with the baggy button-down shirts she always wore with her jeans.

Pickle, on the other hand, would never be called pretty. With unusually deep-set eyes and a nearly black unibrow, a long nose, and a strangely small mouth filled with crooked teeth, Pickle's looks weren't going to open doors for him. He was going to have to rely on his smarts to get him through life. Thankfully, he had plenty of those.

Pickle narrowed his eyes at Julius to deliver the killing blow. "He might have even *stolen* my macros."

"I did not!" Julius erupted. The sound came out as a cross between a honk and a screech.

Ms. Billings pushed a button on her own remote, a remote that controlled at least a dozen robotic creations in the room. Robotic arms attached to a monkey holding cymbals flung the cymbals out and smashed them back together. The metallic clang created a hush in the classroom.

Julius crossed his arms and sulked, but he didn't whine anymore.

Everyone else was still.

After five seconds, Ms. Billings said calmly in her flat, even tone, "Dilbert makes excellent points, Julius. I suggest you attempt to implement some modification strategies of your own. Successful robotics aren't about getting others to make changes so your creation functions properly. We live in a world filled with RF signals. You're going to have to problem-solve the issue using the techniques and knowledge you've learned in this class."

Reed grinned at Julius's red ears. *Smackdown! Ha!*

Reed looked around the room to see if anyone else was enjoying Julius's embarrassment as much as he was. His gaze landed on Leah, a curvy girl with round glasses whom Reed had admired for much of the year. No one ever wanted to talk to her, but her happy demeanor and self-confidence were unshakable. Leah noticed Reed's gaze, and she winked at him. Whether or not the wink was shared enjoyment of Julius's discomfort was unclear. But Reed smiled at her anyway.

The rest of the fifteen kids in the class didn't look toward either Julius or Reed. They were all either fiddling with their projects or looking at Ms. Billings. *Figures.* This class wasn't exactly a cross-section of the normal freshman. Except for Julius, who was an odd combination of jock, brain, and bully, everyone else in the room could have been in the running for Geek of the Year, if there was such a contest. There were more glasses, bad haircuts, and mismatched clothes in this room than in the rest of the school combined. Robotics class might as well be called "Misfits class."

"Now," Ms. Billings said, "if there are no other questions or complaints?"

No one said a word. No one moved.

"Good." Ms. Billings stood and stepped over to the blackboard. "Let's move on to a deeper discussion of actuators. I understand some of you are having problems there. So what are the four common types we talked about last week?"

Shelly's hand shot up. Reed suppressed a grin. Shelly had never met a question she didn't want to answer, and for some reason, he always enjoyed seeing her small square hand with its bitten-to-the-nub fingernails stuck up in the air, vibrating with eagerness. Her excitement was audible through the beaded bracelets she liked to wear; they clacked together while she waited for Ms. Billings to call on her.

"Yes, Shelly?"

"Electric motors, solenoids, hydraulic systems, and pneumatic systems."

"Excellent." While she wrote Shelly's answer on the blackboard with her right hand, Ms. Billings pressed another button on the remote in her left hand. A small spider-shaped skeleton crawled up the inside wall of the classroom and stuck a light-bulb-shaped sticker on the row next to Shelly's name, which was on a huge chart that included all the class's names. Shelly had more stickers than anyone else. Reed had none.

Reed turned away from the stupid chart and looked out the window at the tiny pale green buds on the oak trees outside the school. He wondered if he could see the buds get bigger if he stared at them long enough. Watching trees grow had to be more interesting than this stuff.

One of Ms. Billing's robotic characters started marching up and down each row between the desks. The exoskeleton was vaguely shaped like a horse. Its hoof-like feet clapped against the gray linoleum floor as it pranced past Reed's dirty athletic shoes. Reed was pretty sure the robot was modeling an example of a hydraulic actuator. But maybe it was pneumatic. He probably should've been paying more attention.

How did Ms. Billing expect anyone to pay attention

in this room full of animated characters, exoskeletons, and robotic parts? It was sensory overload, like having class in a circus. On top of that, even though Ms. Billings wore conservative pantsuits, she obviously loved the color red, which was splashed all over the school's institutional pale yellow walls in the form of huge posters and a myriad of charts. It was distracting.

A wadded-up piece of paper landed on Reed's desk, next to his pathetic exoskeleton. He blinked and glanced at Ms. Billings. She had her back to the class, so he spread out the paper. It was a note from Shelly: *Coming home with us? Long homework session!* followed by a smiley face. Shelly thought long homework sessions were fun.

He looked at Shelly. She was watching Ms. Billings, but she nodded when Reed gave her a thumbs-up. Not that he wanted to do homework. But he did want to go home with his friends. And besides, he had to do homework. At least when he studied with Shelly and Pickle, he got better grades.

As soon as Ms. Billings dismissed the class, Pickle grabbed his robot and jumped up. He did this every day because this was the last class before lunch. Pickle loved to eat. That was the only other thing he had going for him: Pickle ate more than Shelly and Reed combined, and he didn't have much more meat on him than his metal skeletal robot did. The boy had the metabolism of a hummingbird.

Today, Pickle was in an even bigger hurry. Today was a half day because all the teachers had some conference to go to. After-school activities had been canceled. There would be no late buses. The principal had announced that morning that the school would be closed up and locked at noon. This meant Pickle and of course Shelly and Reed were in for an afternoon of the great snacks Mrs. Girard put out for the twins and their little brother, Ory, on special days like this. Even on normal days, stuff like homemade pizzas, veggie egg rolls, and grilled sandwiches were typical after-school eats at the Girard house. But on "special days," Mrs. Girard went over the top.

Pickle, Shelly, and their little brother, Ory, were beyond lucky. Their mom was home to make them hot food in the afternoon and then another great meal later on in the evening. Reed was lucky if he could scrounge up a few pretzels when he had to go home to his empty house. Luckily, he usually got to go home with the twins. If he didn't, he'd have been even skinnier than he was.

Pickle started trotting up the aisle toward the door as Reed picked up his project and tried to figure out how to shove it into his backpack. He didn't take his eyes off of Pickle as he folded and refolded the project's robotic arms, so he saw when Julius stuck out his foot and tripped Pickle.

Pickle, who wasn't the most coordinated kid anyway,

lost his balance and flew forward into the desk in front of Julius. Pickle's big nose led the way wherever his face went, so his nose took the brunt of the impact when it hit the corner of the desk. Blood spurted from Pickle's nostrils as Julius snorted out a high-pitched laugh.

Ms. Billings, who had been gathering a stack of books and preparing to leave the room, didn't see a thing. Neither did anyone else. Everyone was too focused on where they were going. Even Shelly had her head down as she collapsed her dog-size exoskeleton into a puppy-size one. This was a particularly clever part of her project, Reed thought. She'd told him if she could figure out how to downsize Thales, too, without hurting him of course, she'd patent "collapsible dogs" and become a billionaire.

Reed's muscles bunched as he watched his friend try to stop the spurting blood with one hand. Reed wanted to help Pickle, and he wanted to confront Julius, but he knew where it would lead if he put himself in the middle. As if reading Reed's mind, Julius turned and smiled.

Julius's unusually pointed canine teeth seemed to gleam under the classroom's fluorescent lighting. Not for the first time, Reed fantasized that Julius was a vampire who could be vaporized by a stake through the heart.

If Julius had a heart.

Reed clenched his fists as Pickle ran from the room,

clutching his robot with one hand and his bloody nose with the other. Before Reed could tell Shelly what had just happened, she got her act together and hurried after Pickle, calling, "Pickle, wait up."

Julius gave Reed the evil eye for another few seconds. Then he turned to gather up his floppy exoskeleton. All the other kids filed out of the room. Reed lingered. He wanted to say something to Julius. What was it Shelly had called Julius the other day, when they were talking about him? *Oh yeah.* She'd said he was an ignominious, odious reprobate. Reed mentally repeated the words. They sounded ridiculous. Only Shelly could get away with saying something like that.

"What're you staring at?" Julius asked Reed.

Reed looked around. He realized he and Julius were alone in the room. He hated that his palms had started sweating and his breathing was coming faster. Why did he let Julius get to him?

Julius stopped trying to gather up his suit. Instead, he carefully laid it out. He grinned at Reed. "Bet you wish you could build something like this, huh, moron?"

Reed didn't answer. He wanted to pick up his backpack and leave, but something kept him in the room. What? He didn't know. It sure wasn't the company, which sucked. It wasn't the decor, which he found intimidating. And it wasn't the smell, which was a cross between chalk and soldering.

"I don't even know what you're doing in this class,"

Julius sneered. "I mean, your runty little friend may be a mini-freak, but at least he has a few brain cells. And your other friend, that weird hair-chewing chick, is an uppity cow, but with a little makeup, she wouldn't be bad to look at. And she has brain cells, too. You've got nothing going for you. You're a freak and nothing can make you worth looking at. And on top of that, you're all air up there, aren't you?" Julius leaned forward and flicked a finger between Reed's eyes.

Reed tightened his fists, and Julius noticed.

"What're you going to do? Hit me? Didn't you see what I did to your pickled friend?" Julius laughed his beyond-annoying laugh. "I didn't even have to lift a finger. I just moved my foot, and now he has a bloody nose. Just think of what I could do to you without giving it much effort."

Reed swallowed. Julius had just called Reed an ugly, stupid freak. And yet, Reed was still standing there as if he couldn't talk.

Reed hated being called a freak, and he hated being called ugly.

Yeah, Reed was a bit of an outcast. When his mom had died, he hadn't seen the point in trying to get along with anyone. He'd separated himself from his friends, using his overwhelming grief as the fence to erect a barrier between himself and the world. Only Pickle and Shelly had bothered to climb the fence.

And no, Reed wasn't much to look at. The truth

was, he was not unlike Pickle in the looks department. Skinny, with unusually long arms, his pronounced brow ridge and jutting jaw gave him more of an apelike appearance than he wanted to admit. More than once, Julius called him "monkey face" when he was younger. Now that his dad let him grow his curly brown hair long, he was able to disguise his primate features a little.

If only he had an ape's strength.

He still wanted to say something to Julius. No, forget saying something. He wanted to *do* something. But he couldn't.

Why did he think things would be any different in high school than they had been in grade school?

Julius lifted his exoskeleton. "See this here? I was going to use it to be stronger and faster, but I don't need to be stronger and faster. I'm already strong and fast. I've figured out a better use. I'm going to get this thing working perfectly, and I'm going to hold you down and put you into it. Then I'll control the exoskeleton, and it will make you do whatever I command it to do. You'll have to be my servant. I'm going to make you wait on me all day long. You'll carry my books. Tie my shoes. Get me my food. Clean up after me. I'm even going to make you dance for me. What do you think about that, loser? Would you like to dance like a monkey for me?"

Reed still didn't speak. It was like he'd been turned to stone. All he could do was stand there and watch Julius lean over and tinker with his exoskeleton. Julius looked up and laughed at Reed. "Cat got your tongue?"

Julius lifted up his exoskeleton suit. "Wanna see it in action? It's pretty amazing, if I do say so myself."

Julius began fitting the suit to his long limbs and V-shaped torso. The metal shell lay over Julius's limbs. A shoulder strap, chest strap, and hip strap, along with clamps at the wrists and ankles, kept everything in place. Reed, biting the inside of his cheek hard enough to draw blood, remained rooted to the spot, watching.

Outside the classroom, students laughed and called to each other as they headed to the buses lined up outside the school. Inside the classroom, it was nearly silent, except for the clicks and snaps of Julius fitting himself into his robotic skeleton.

"See here?" Julius held up his arms. He indicated his wrists, then pointed to his ankles. "I've equipped the exoskeleton with locking mechanisms so once I get you in it, I can keep you in it."

Reed watched Julius struggle with some of the joints of his exoskeleton. Julius shifted the framework on his body, then adjusted the suit's piston cylinders.

Outside, a couple buses started their engines, and a baritone rumbling vibrated the walls of the school. If Reed didn't leave soon, he'd have to walk to the Girards' house. He'd have to walk over seven miles . . . all because he'd stood here like a paralyzed mute for the last several minutes. He shook his head to try and get his brain rebooted.

Julius, heavy with the exoskeleton riding his body, leaned down and fiddled with the wires leading to the skeleton's circuits. Reed wished he had the guts to reach out and shove Julius across the room, him and his stupid exoskeleton.

But it was a good thing he didn't.

A second later, Reed was glad he wasn't touching Julius.

A radiant flash burst up like fireworks as a power surge sparked in the exoskeleton. Julius's body twitched. His eyes widened, and he went rigid for several seconds.

In those seconds, Reed's mind bizarrely thought of the previous day's word of the day. Shelly shared every one of them with him. He forgot most of them, but he remembered *fulgurant*, which meant "flashing like lightning." *That power surge was fulgurant*, he thought.

With curiosity for what was going to happen next, Reed watched the stiffness leave Julius's body. Julius wavered on his feet, lost his balance, and fell back on his desk. Shaking his head, he groped for his chair and slid into it. He put his head down, and for what felt like a long twenty seconds, Julius was perfectly still.

Was he alive?

Reed blinked and studied Julius's inert form. Then Reed's gaze landed on the wrist and ankle joints of the suit.

Finally, Reed moved. Stepping over to Julius, Reed quickly locked the wrist and ankle joints. They fitted together with a satisfying *snick*. As soon as they did, Reed stepped back and grinned.

That would teach the ignominious odious reprobate.

Reed picked up his backpack and slung it over his shoulder. He watched as Julius opened his eyes. It took a second for him to get oriented, but when he did, he attempted to strip off the exoskeleton.

"Oops," Reed said. He backed toward the classroom door. He finally found his voice. "I must have locked you in. My bad."

Julius jerked his arms, yanking to free them from the restraints of his skeletal suit. He kicked his legs. With his right hand, he grabbed at the exoskeleton hugging his left hand. He grunted and strained. The skeleton wouldn't budge.

"What the hell did you do, punk?" Julius yelled. "Unlock me!"

"I don't think so," Reed said.

"Do what I tell you! Unlock me!" Julius's face was a mottled mix of red and purple, and his eyes looked like they were bulging out of his head. Spittle clung to the corners of his mouth.

Reed shrugged and grinned. He couldn't remember the last time he was this pleased with himself.

Not that he'd thought through what he was doing. What was the point of what he'd just done? Was he just messing with Julius or was he going to leave Julius in the suit overnight? Could he do that?

Why not?

He'd get in trouble was why not. Julius would tell the teachers what Reed did.

But all Reed would have to do was deny it. If he made sure Julius was unlocked by morning, why would anyone suspect Reed of anything? Everyone knew he was pretty much a wuss. No one would believe he'd had the courage to do this.

"Unlock me!" Julius commanded again. The muscles in his neck stood out like cords. His jaw jutted, and he kept opening and closing his fists.

At this point, Reed really had no choice but to leave Julius here all night. If he let Julius out now, Julius was going to beat the crap out of him. Even if he unlocked Julius and ran, Reed probably wouldn't outrun the guy. Julius was crazy fast, and Reed was an athletic spaz. If he waited until morning, there would be enough people around that Julius wouldn't touch him.

The decision basically made itself. Julius was going to be locked in overnight. The idea buoyed Reed so much, he felt like he was floating.

"I'm going to do you a favor," Reed said, happy that he had something clever to say. "I'm going to leave you here in your suit overnight so you can get an idea of what it feels like to have someone treat you the way you treat everyone else. Maybe your robot can teach you a thing or two."

"Hey!" Julius tried to get up, but his exoskeleton was

contracted and stiff. It was acting like a full body cast, keeping Julius's body locked in a seated position.

"Have fun," Reed called as he sprinted from the room. Before he left the classroom, he shut off the lights.

"Get back here, you stupid ape!" Julius screamed. "Do you know what you've done? I'm going to kill you!" The last few words came out as a nearly unintelligible screech as Reed pulled the door closed.

Julius began bellowing. "I'm going to rip your head off and flush it down the toilet. I'm going to tear you apart, limb from limb. Get back in here and unlock this!"

Reed laughed. For some reason, Julius's threats, which normally would have reduced Reed to quivering jelly, sounded funny. For once, Julius had no power. Reed had it all.

Reed looked around the empty hallway. He was alone. Good. This whole wing was probably empty by now. As an auxiliary hall near the back of the school, it wasn't used outside of class hours. No one would find Julius even if he yelled his head off.

"Come back here and let me out of this thing!" Julius screamed. "You can't leave me in here like this!"

Reed grinned. Then he turned and ran through the school, hoping he wasn't too late to catch his bus.

Because Mr. Janson, the bus driver, was always looking out for him, Reed didn't miss his bus. He made a total fool of himself waving his arms around and shouting as

Mr. Janson started to pull away from the curb, but he got the driver's attention.

Mr. Janson stopped the bus a few feet from the curb and opened the bus's doors. The driver of one of the buses farther down the row behind Reed's bus honked. Stumbling up the stairs into the bus, Reed gasped, "Thanks," to Mr. Janson, who shook his gray-haired head and winked at Reed. "Cutting it close, my boy. Cutting it close."

Reed sucked in some air. "Sorry."

"Life happens," Mr. Janson said. "We adjust." He smiled at Reed. "Take your seat."

Reed scanned the interior of the bus. One of the cheerleaders gave him a disgusted look. Reed ignored her and looked for Shelly and Pickle. He knew they'd be at the back of the bus, and he knew they'd saved him a seat. Keeping his gaze on his feet and the aisle's scuffed rubber flooring, Reed hurried to his friends. He slid in next to Pickle.

As soon as Reed's butt hit the hard maroon vinyl seat, Mr. Janson released the brakes. The bus hissed, lurched, and rumbled away from the school.

Reed looked at Pickle's nose. It was hard not to. Red and swollen, smeared with blood, Pickle's nose was more prominent than ever, and now he had little white tissue rolls sticking out of each nostril. Given that his nose was beaky, Pickle looked like a big bird sucking up white worms.

"Does it hurt?" Reed asked.

Pickle, as usual, was doing some kind of numbers puzzle. He glanced up at Reed. "Huh?"

Reed pointed at his nose.

Pickle made a funny cross-eyed face in an attempt to look at his injured beak. Reed suppressed a smile.

Pickle shrugged. "Yeah. Not the first time, though. I can ignore it."

"Sorry."

"Why? What did you do?"

"Nothing."

Pickle returned to his puzzle.

Reed glanced at Shelly. She was reading, also as usual.

The bus smelled like diesel exhaust, sweat, peanuts, and bubble gum. Its engine sounded like the contented snore of a sleeping dragon. The sound helped tension and adrenaline drain from Reed's system.

The bus gained speed as it turned out of the school's driveway onto the road. Reed looked out the window.

The high school was tucked into the back of an older neighborhood, so the first few blocks after they left the school were full of big trees and pretty green lawns. Reed usually liked looking at all that greenery. He would stare at the lawns with envy. His front yard was mostly dirt.

Today, Reed wasn't really seeing anything he was looking at. He was back in the robotics classroom with

Julius. His mind was focused on Julius locked into his exoskeleton, Julius's face nearly purple with rage.

"'In the dark ages,'" Shelly said, "'harsh torture was commonly used to punish those who broke the law.'"

Reed flinched. "What?"

He turned to stare at Shelly. As always, she sat in the seat behind Pickle and Reed. Her massive backpack and extra book bag took up the rest of the seat.

Did she know what he'd done?

Her attention on her book, Shelly continued, "'When someone violated civil law, torture would be done in the town square. Public display of the consequences for lawlessness was thought to be a deterrent.'"

Oh. She was reading. Of course she was. She loved to share what she was learning, and she often read aloud on the bus . . . and at home . . . and at lunch . . . and in the hallways at school—she read pretty much everywhere. Today, she was reading her history homework. Shelly was in AP World History because she'd read so many history books outside of school that she was beyond the normal history curriculum. She wasn't just a science geek. She was an information geek.

Reed relaxed his shoulders and returned his attention to the window. When it left behind the neighborhood, the bus route ran along a main drag lined with strip malls and car dealerships. Reed liked this stretch, too, because he enjoyed looking at the cars. He liked to imagine himself driving them, and he picked a different make and model every day. Concentrating, he put himself at the wheel of a new bright yellow Mustang.

Shelly's voice, however, ruined his fantasy.

"'Torturers were very creative in the middle ages,'" Shelly read. "'They came up with truly morbid ways of inflicting excruciating pain. The Judas Cradle, for example, impaled a seated victim for several days. With bloodcurdling names like the Breast Ripper and the Pear of Anguish, medieval torture devices were a testament to human ingenuity.'"

Torture. Was what I did to Julius torture?

Reed's chest tightened. Yeah, it probably was. Being stuck was at least a mild form of torture, especially in an exoskeleton with no way to move or eat or drink or get to the bathroom. It wasn't the Judas Cradle, but it wasn't nice, either.

After the malls and car lots, their bus route wound through an industrial park, and then it passed a farm before turning into a newer subdivision. Most of the bus's stops were in this subdivision, which was stuffed full of houses that, though good-size, mostly looked alike. Reed didn't care about the houses, so he stopped registering individual things. Now he saw just blurs of color . . . and Julius stuck in that metal framework.

Reed's dad, who did the best he could to be a single dad to Reed and his sister, Alexa, was fond of saying that you couldn't solve a problem at the level of the problem. Reed wasn't a genius like his friends, but he was smart enough to know that meant that lowering himself to the level of Julius's meanness wasn't the way to handle the jerk.

But still, after what Julius did to Pickle? Wasn't that justification enough to lock Julius into the exoskeleton he was so proud of? And what about what Julius said to Reed, about locking Reed into the exoskeleton? Didn't Julius deserve to get a taste of his own medicine?

Reed started to unwind his muscles again.

Yeah. What he did wasn't so bad. It was justice.

The bus went through a pothole, and everyone popped up off their seats for a nanosecond. When they all landed again, Shelly poked Reed's shoulder. He turned to look at her.

"Listen to this," she said. "You won't believe it."

"What?" Reed asked.

Pickle said nothing. He kept inking in the answers to his puzzle.

"'One of the most commonly used forms of torture was called the Wheel,'" Shelly read from her thick, musty-smelling book. "'Those condemned to being constrained in this way had prolonged torture ahead of them. They were held in place, unable to free themselves.'"

Reed stared at Shelly. What was she doing? Was she messing with him? *Held in place, unable to free themselves.* It sounded like she was talking about Julius. Maybe she knew what he'd done after all. But how?

"'It was sometimes called the Breaking Wheel,'" Shelly read on.

Reed blew out air. No, she didn't know what he'd done. It was just a coincidence that she was reading about torture devices.

"'They called it that,'" she continued, "'because it was used to crush the bones of the condemned.' Ew, huh?" Shelly looked at Reed with wide eyes. Then she returned her gaze to the book and read on. "'The device was designed for torture lasting over multiple days. The Wheel was made up of many radial spokes, and the person subjected to it was tied to the whole wheel before a club or cudgel was used to beat their limbs. This process reduced the human being into a mutilated bag of bones, what one onlooker described as a writhing, moaning monster with bloody tentacles.'"

"That's gross," Pickle said without looking up from his puzzle.

"Totally," Reed agreed. He tried not to think about what Julius was experiencing now.

But hey, at least Julius wasn't tied to a medieval torture device, right?

Julius was restrained, and as time passed, he'd be uncomfortable. But he wasn't in any pain. No one was standing over him beating him with a cudgel, whatever that was. He was just trapped.

Shelly continued to read about medieval torture, but Reed tuned her out. He turned back toward the window.

The bus was stopped at a corner, and he watched a mom holding hands with a little kid who held a red balloon. The balloon bobbed in the air, following the little kid's movements because it was tied to the kid's wrist.

Reed thought about Julius's big wrists. Maybe he should go back to the school and unlock the exoskeleton after their study session this evening. A few hours would be enough to punish Julius for his nastiness. That way, Julius would learn his lesson, but Reed wouldn't stoop to the level of torture.

Yeah, that's what Reed would do.

Except, how would he get away from Julius before Julius tried to kill him?

Reed chewed on his lower lip.

He sat up straight and smiled. He knew what he could do. He'd unlock just one of Julius's hands, then jump back and run before Julius could grab him. Julius, stiff from his confinement, would take at least half a minute to unlock his other wrist and his ankles, and in that time, Reed could get far enough away to hide. Once Julius was gone, Reed could go home.

And after that?

Well, he'd deal with that when the time came.

But until then, he was going to have some good food at the Girards' house and hang out with his friends. He was going to put Julius out of his mind and enjoy the rest of his free time that day. He deserved it.

Just like Julius deserved what was happening to him.

★ ★ ★

Reed loved his dad, and he knew his dad did everything he could to give Reed and Alexa a good home, but his dad was, well, his dad. He knew nothing about what a good home was. He couldn't cook. He couldn't clean. He thought "decoration" was a calendar with fish photos on it and a few sport teams' schedules. When Reed was home, he never really felt at home, not like he did here at the Girard house.

Reed sprawled on a thick, soft gray rug in front of a stone hearth. A low-burning fire sputtered on the grate. Thales, exhausted from a rousing game of chase-the-tennis-ball, was now stretched out on the cool tiles of the nearby entryway, adding his satisfied snores to the flames' staccato popping. The sounds were both rhythmic and soothing.

Reed's belly was full of spicy chicken wings, jalapeno poppers, potato skins, homemade potpie, and chocolate cookies. He was so relaxed he wished he could take a nap.

"You kids have everything you need before I head to my class?" Mrs. Girard asked. She stood in the archway between the family room and the entryway, tugging on a floppy yellow rain hat.

Reed turned and looked over his shoulder, out through the French doors to the Girards' heavily treed backyard. Yep. It was raining, a steady but light spring rain. The drops looked shiny and pink in the twilight. Reed craned his neck to see the Western horizon. He liked looking at the sun when it was getting ready to slide into nighttime. Tonight, the sun was a fuzzy bright orange tinged with purple.

He looked back at Mrs. Girard. "Thanks for the snacks and for dinner, too."

Mrs. Girard smiled and tucked her shoulder-length dark hair under the rain hat. She shrugged her short, plump body into her slicker, and said, "You're welcome, as always, Reed. We love having you here." She snapped her slicker closed and looked at her own kids, who were all oblivious of her impending departure.

Shelly, reclining on an overstuffed navy-blue sofa, had her nose buried in the same thick history book she'd been reading on the bus. Pickle sat cross-legged in his dad's blue tweed recliner, bending so low over his own book it looked like he was trying to dive into it. Reed couldn't see what Pickle was reading. The third Girard kid, six-year-old Ory, had been playing a video game, but now he was picking up the remote for Pickle's robot skeleton.

"Kids!" Mrs. Girard yelled.

All three of her children looked up.

Mrs. Girard shook her head and smiled. "I'm leaving. You kids behave. And, Pickle, ice that nose again in an hour or so."

"Huh?" Pickle said.

Mrs. Girard shook her head.

"I'll remind him," Reed said.

Pickle's nose was looking much better. Predictably, Mrs. Girard had matter-of-factly treated Pickle's nose the second they got home. Examining it, she'd declared it "bruised, not broken," and she'd cleaned it up, applied some kind of herbal cream, and then given Pickle an ice pack to balance on his face. Pickle resisted that because he couldn't eat or read with the pack on his nose. But he didn't have to leave it on for long. Soon, he was eating snacks along with everyone else. And he declared the double chocolate cookies Mrs. Girard brought out after dinner "healing cookies" because his nose stopped hurting after he ate them.

Now, after studying her beaky son for a second, Mrs. Girard looked at Reed. "What would we do without you, Reed?" Mrs. Girard smiled at him and then turned her back to her kids. "Bye, kids."

"Love you, Mom," Shelly said.

"Bye," Pickle and Ory said in unison.

"Thanks again, Mrs. Girard. Bye," Reed said.

"Bye, all," Mrs. Girard said. "Come on, Thales."

Thales was already on his feet, standing next to Mrs. Girard's legs. His tail whipped so fast it was slapping her in the thigh. Mrs. Girard's class was his class, too. He was learning to be a therapy dog.

Mrs. Girard, though not the source of her children's brilliance, was no brain slouch. She went to all sorts of classes. She seemed to have a lot of interests, and she always joined in the conversations when her kids were babbling on about their homework or projects. But the Girard brains came mostly from Mr. Girard. He was a retired electrical engineer who now did consulting for big companies. He traveled a lot, and he was gone now, but when he was here, he was a hands-on dad. He was cool.

Shelly and Pickle had returned to their books before the front door shut behind Mrs. Girard. Ory pressed a button on the remote control, and Pickle's robot skeleton stood up and slid forward a few inches. Ory's eyes lit up.

Ory was a conglomeration of his siblings, which made him not as cute as Shelly but much cuter than Pickle. His face still round and a little pudgy, Ory had Shelly's large eyes and long lashes and full mouth. And he had his brother's nose. On Ory, the big nose was more amusing than ugly. He looked a little like a baby bird. Six-year-olds could rock a look like that. Ory wouldn't have to worry about looks for a while.

Ory bent over the remote, so intent on it, he nearly touched it with his long nose. The little robot skeleton scooted forward some more. Ory laughed.

Reed glanced at Pickle. Pickle either didn't know his brother was playing with his project or he didn't care. Probably if Ory damaged the thing in any way, Pickle could easily fix it.

Reed looked at his own pathetic project. He was supposed to be working on it. And he had been, sort of, off and on all afternoon. He hadn't made much progress, though.

Reed had chosen an electric motor as his actuator because his dad knew how to build a motor and was excited to help him. That part of the project, along with connecting the battery-powered motor to the exoskeleton's circuitry, had gone okay. The problem Reed had now was with the skeleton's structure. As always, he couldn't visualize how to construct the form. Every time he attached a new metal component to the skeleton, he ended up with something that stuck out at an unnatural angle. And when he turned it to make it fit, the joint didn't work properly. Right now, his exoskeleton looked mangled and backward. This wasn't good.

Reed sighed and gazed around the cozy room. Even though the Girard family room was big and had high ceilings, it was warm and inviting, kind of like a cocoon. Filled with comfortable soft furniture, a couple tables, multiple shelves stuffed with books and games, colorful art, a tidy play area for Ory, a big microfiber-covered bed for Thales, the fireplace, and a huge TV for movie night and video games, the room was perfect for hanging out. It wasn't so bad for doing homework, either. You might as well be comfortable while you were doing something you didn't want to do.

The week before, the family room got an addition

that intrigued Reed. It was a miniature house, a replica of the Girard home. Standing about three feet tall and stretching four feet wide, the house required the removal of one ottoman from the room. But otherwise, it fit in just fine. Mr. Girard built the house for Shelly, and she was decorating it to look exactly like the family's real house.

"Do you want me to help you with that?" Pickle asked.

"Huh?" Reed looked over at his friend.

Pickle marked his book, which Reed could now see was on advanced engineering mathematics. "You sighed," Pickle said, "and your exoskeleton looks like it's being built by a blind man without opposable thumbs. I wondered if you wanted some help."

Reed threw a gear at Pickle. Pickle didn't mean to be mean . . . he was just brilliant in his own, matter-of-fact kind of way. That was why he was okay to hang out with even though he was super smart. Pickle never made Reed feel dumb, even when he made a comment like that one. Reed knew Pickle wasn't making fun of him. Pickle was just making an observation. "I'll muddle through, thank you."

"You might try angling the joints so the left and right limbs move in the same, or at least similar, ways . . . unless you're building an alien exoskeleton."

"Thank you, Mr. Obvious," Reed said. He made a face. "Maybe I am building an alien exoskeleton."

"Cool." Pickle shrugged and returned to his book.

Shelly looked up from hers. "What?"

Reed laughed. "My exoskeleton is an alien."

Shelly rolled her eyes and returned to reading.

Ory laughed. Reed turned to see if the kid was laughing at Reed. He wasn't. He was fully focused on the robot's remote.

Pickle's robotic skeleton plowed into the hearth with a loud *crunch*. Pickle didn't look up from his book. Ory backed up the seven-inch skeleton and started spinning it in a circle.

Reed began to reconsider Pickle's offer. He was pretty sure Pickle had built his little robotic skeleton in a day. Maybe he could help Reed salvage his project.

Seriously, look at the thing move, Reed thought. He shook his head at the little robotic skeleton as it whipped in tight circles.

He sucked in his breath and sat up. How could he have forgotten what happened in class today?

Well, to be fair, a lot had happened since class. The confrontation with Julius, along with Reed's resulting uncharacteristic burst of nerve, had pretty much acted like a brain wipe of the rest of the day. All Reed could think about was Julius locked in his exoskeleton.

But now he remembered! Julius had been complaining that Pickle's remote was affecting Julius's exoskeleton.

And Julius was now locked into that metal frame, his

body inextricably linked with its structure and therefore inextricably linked with its movement. What if it had crashed into something the way Pickle's robot had just crashed into the hearth? What if it was spinning in circles right now?

"Hey, Pickle?" Reed kept his gaze on the gyrating mini metal skeleton.

"Huh?" Pickle looked up at Reed.

"That thing"—Reed pointed at the remote in Ory's small hands—"doesn't have much of a range, right?"

Pickle sniffed. "It's a pretty great range, actually. I designed the remote to function through walls. That's why I combined IR and RF."

"So, if it was controlling, um, something, outside the house, how far would its range be?" Reed asked.

Pickle frowned. "You mean if the skeleton was outside and Ory was inside?"

Reed nodded. "Yeah."

Sure, that's what he meant. He didn't mean *if the remote was controlling Julius's exoskeleton?* No, he didn't mean that at all.

Pickle tilted his head and thought about it. "It might reach to a few feet outside the house. Maybe. Honestly, I've never checked. It probably doesn't reach beyond the house. The outer walls would be thicker than the inside walls. More interference."

"Oh," Reed said, attempting to sound uninterested, even though he had asked the question. "Okay."

Reed tugged at his T-shirt, which was sticking to his suddenly sweaty skin. He suppressed a sigh of relief.

Pickle leaned forward. "Why'd you ask?"

Ory now had the robotic skeleton racing through the room in dizzying serpentine routes around furniture. Reed tried not to imagine Julius zipping around the robotics classroom in a similar fashion. If he was doing in his suit what Pickle's robot was doing here, Julius would be bashed into walls and furniture. He'd be, at the least, badly bruised. More likely, he'd have broken bones.

Oh man, Reed thought, *I might be truly torturing Julius!*

"Reed?"

Reed looked at Pickle. He was suddenly elated that his friend's genius didn't extend to reading minds. And he was also glad that Pickle also sucked at deciphering facial expressions, body language, and other social cues. Reed was sure his deliberately blank face wasn't as effective as he wanted it to be. He was trying for innocent, but he had a feeling he looked like Thales did when the dog stole a cookie and was trying to pretend he didn't.

"Oh, I was just curious," Reed said. "It's impressive. That's all."

Pickle raised a thick black eyebrow. "Okay."

Pickle might not have been able to read interpersonal visual cues, but his brain was like an audio recorder.

He remembered everything he'd ever read or heard. He was now going through that database and contrasting everything Reed had ever said to him before today with what Reed had just said.

Reed had never before told Pickle that something he'd done was impressive. He was so used to Pickle outperforming everyone around him that praising Pickle for doing something well was sort of like praising him for breathing. Pickle definitely found Reed's last comment strange.

Pickle opened his mouth as if he was going to ask a question, but Ory saved Reed. He plowed Pickle's exoskeleton into the side of Shelly's miniature house.

The metal hit the wood siding with a *thud*, and Shelly sat up on the sofa. She stuck a bookmark in her book, clearly ready to confront her little brother. Before she could do or say anything, though, Ory backed up the robotic skeleton and ran it forward again. He giggled and repeated the action, bumping the little robot into the miniature house over and over.

Shelly jumped up. "Hey! Ory, stop it!"

"He's not going to hurt it," Pickle said. "Let him play with it."

"I'm not worried about your robot," Shelly said. "He's going to hurt my house. He's going to mess up my project." Shelly started toward Ory, who giggled and darted away from her. Shelly chased Ory, but he easily stayed ahead of her. He continued to play with the remote at the same time, so the little robot kept butting at the house.

"Ory, you little twerp," Shelly said, "I'm going to break our sibling vinculum if you don't cut that out."

Vinculum was one of the daily words from the previous week. It meant "bond." That one stuck in Reed's head because he thought, when Shelly defined the word, that he'd like a deeper vinculum with her.

"Ory! If you ruin my project . . ."

"What project?" Reed asked. He didn't care. He was trying to distract himself from thoughts about Julius, who, if he was being controlled by Pickle's remote, was probably being slammed into a wall in the classroom right now.

Or what if he was being slammed into something sharp, like one of Ms. Billings's robotic arms? Could Julius get impaled?

"It's a project for psychology class, about family dynamics," Shelly said, panting and lunging for her little brother.

"Seriously, Shel, it's okay," Pickle said. "The robot isn't going to hurt the house. It doesn't have any sharp edges." Pickle set aside his book and scrambled out of his dad's chair. He went over to where his robot was attacking the house over and over. Leaning forward and pointing at the tiny rough pieces of overlapping wood that looked like the gray shingled siding on the real house, he said, "See? Not a scratch."

Shelly stopped pursuing Ory. She came back to the miniature house, knelt down, and examined it. "Oh." She shrugged and returned to the sofa. "Okay." She picked up her book and presumably returned to medieval torture.

Torture.

What if Julius was being tortured right now? He had to be battered pretty badly if he'd been forced to do everything Pickle's robot was doing.

Pickle sat down on the floor in front of Shelly's house. He reached out and snatched up his robot. "Ory, desist for a second."

Ory shoved out his lower lip. "But, I wanna . . . ," he began to whine.

"I'm not going to take it away from you," Pickle assured his brother. "I'm going to make it more fun." Pickle held up his metal skeleton, which was still whirring in an effort to respond to the remote's commands.

Ory's lower lip returned to its normal position. He stopped playing with the remote, and his face brightened. "Yeah? What're you going to do?" He came over and sat down next to Pickle.

"I've got something cool to show you," Pickle said. "It's something else you can do with this."

Pickle put down the robot. He nudged Ory. "So, watch this," Pickle whispered. Pickle flipped a switch on the little robot.

"Now, try it," Pickle said to Ory.

Ory grinned and pushed a button on the remote. The robot stood on its blockish head.

"What'd you just do?" Reed asked Pickle.

"Oh, I just turned off the joint constraints. So now, my robot can go against logical joint directions, too. Like yours, only on purpose."

Ory gleefully pushed buttons and toggled the joystick on the remote, and the little robot flipped off its head and turned into a metal contortionist. It started crawling across the floor like an octopus, its joints warping into impossible pretzel-like shapes. Looking at once like it was turning itself inside out and like it was expanding and contracting the way a beating heart did, the robot became so fluid it resembled a snake.

Ory directed the robot into the entry area, and it clicked and clacked over the slate as it undulated across the floor. Reed stared at it, his throat constricting.

In his head, instead of the sound of the robot's metal limbs contacting the hard floor, Reed could hear the snaps and pops of breaking bones . . . Julius's breaking bones. The sounds were in his head, weren't they? He was imagining it and not hearing it, right?

No, of course he wasn't hearing it. How could he hear it? Pickle said the remote's range wouldn't reach much beyond the Girards' house, and even if it was happening, Reed wouldn't be able to hear it. His ears weren't superhuman. They were miles from the school. If his mind was telling him he could hear Julius's bones break, his mind was lying.

Reed's fears were so stupid. He couldn't believe his mind was coming up with this stuff. It was asinine. There was no way Pickle's remote could have any impact on Julius's framework. Therefore, it was having no impact on Julius.

So why did Reed feel so rotten? Why was his stomach in his throat? Why did he feel like he might throw up all the great food he'd eaten?

Did he intuitively know something? Was his intuition right and his logic wrong?

Reed took a deep breath and looked at his exoskeleton. *Focus*, he told himself. *Stop imagining all that stupid stuff.*

Reed leaned over his project. He tried to concentrate on his exoskeleton's joints.

But he couldn't. Ory was having just too much fun with Pickle's robot. Now that the boy could make the thing writhe all over the place, he was practically dancing with glee.

Pickle returned to his dad's easy chair and picked up his book. Shelly was still lost in her own reading.

Ory started making the robot assault Shelly's house again. Shelly glanced up, but apparently comforted by Pickle's assurances, she placidly returned to her book.

Reed scrambled off the floor. He'd had enough.

"I'll be back," he said. "I have to do something."

Ory ignored him, continuing to aim the flopping robot at the side of Shelly's house. Pickle looked up from his book. "Where are you going?"

"I have to do something," Reed repeated.

"What?" Pickle asked.

What could Reed say?

He couldn't say, "I have to go to the school and free Julius," even though that was exactly what he had to do. He had to run the three blocks to his house, get his bike, and pedal back to the school. Then he had to get in the locked school without setting off an alarm . . . thankfully he'd overheard a senior talking about a basement door that wasn't wired into the school's security system, and a key ring the janitor kept in a fake rock. Then he had to go through the darkened school without wetting his pants like a scared little kid, and then he had to unlock Julius and run for his life.

No, wait. Should he check on Julius before running?

What if his worst fears were true?

If Julius was badly injured, wouldn't Reed have to call an ambulance?

He almost groaned out loud, but he stopped himself.

And what if Julius was dead?

"Reed?"

Reed blinked when he realized Pickle had said his name.

"What?" he said.

"You said you had to do something," Pickle reminded

him. "I asked what you had to do. Then your brain took a vacation and you turned into a weird statue."

"Statue?" Reed was stalling.

He tried to think of a reasonable story. What would he have to do right now? Other than go save Julius from a modern-day version of the Wheel?

"Shelly?" Pickle said. "I think something's wrong with Reed."

Shelly looked up from her book. "Of course something's wrong with Reed," she said. "He doesn't engage in enough intellection, and he lacks the appropriate nisus when it comes to schoolwork."

Oh snap, Reed thought. Even in his agitated state, he recognized that Shelly had just used two words of the day. However, he was far too distracted to care about what they meant.

"I'm not talking about Reed's commonplace imperfections," Pickle said. "I'm referring to the fact that he's currently making no sense and his body keeps forgetting how to remain animated."

"Well, see, that's what I like about Reed," Shelly said.

Reed perked up, momentarily forgetting everything but finding out what Shelly liked about him.

"What's that?" Pickle asked.

Reed was relieved he didn't have to be the one who asked.

"He rarely makes sense. I like that. It gives me a challenge and keeps me interested."

Reed couldn't stop himself. He grinned like a maniac.

Thankfully, no one was looking at him. Pickle and Shelly were looking at each other. Ory's gaze was on the little robot, whose metal limbs were now so distorted they looked elastic.

"I can see your point," Pickle said to Shelly. "But my original question remains." Pickle returned his attention to Reed. "What do you have to do?"

Before Reed could come up with something lame, the little robot hit the side of the miniature house again. And when it did, something large hit the outside of the Girards' house.

Shelly looked at the French doors, then put her attention back on her book. "Wind must have come up."

"We probably lost another branch off the big fir tree," Pickle said.

Reed looked at the window.

In the short time since Mrs. Girard had left, night had slipped in around the house. Now blackness clung to the windows like a fungus. Reed couldn't see anything in the framed glass of the French doors except the reflection of the room he was in. In that reflection, he watched Ory aim the robot at the house again. He watched it hit the miniature house.

In the same instant, something hit the side of the house again with a reverberating *thump*. Reed tensed. He looked at his friends.

Neither Pickle nor Shelly reacted to the latest sound. They were apparently satisfied with the wind-and-fallen-branch explanation for the second *thump*. Or, since they were reading again, they may not have even heard it.

Well, Reed heard it, and the wind explanation didn't cut it.

He was listening intently now, and even though he'd heard those impacts against the house, what he didn't hear was wind strong enough to blow a branch at the house that could make noise. He should've been hearing a whistling, whooshing sound if the wind was blowing that hard. And except for the continued crackle in the fireplace, and the sound of the robot hitting Shelly's little house, the only other things Reed could hear were the impacts on the side of the house ... every time the robotic skeleton hit the model house.

What if it was Julius out there?

What if he truly had been manipulated by Pickle's remote all this time? By now, what condition would Julius be in?

What Reed lacked in "intellection" he made up for in imagination. He could easily envision a body covered in swelling, blackened contusions. He could see limbs as limp as rubber with bone fragments poking through the skin. He could see a battered face, a bleeding skull, and a spine warped into something sickeningly abnormal.

If, in his exoskeleton, Julius had been spun, then

bashed into things over and over, and if he'd been twisted and contorted the way Pickle's robot had been, would Julius even be human anymore? He'd be a mutilated mass of broken bones and torn flesh. What was it Shelly's history book had said about the victims of the Wheel?

A victim of the wheel ended up looking like a moaning monster with bloody tentacles.

Yep. That's what Julius would have become if everything Ory had done to Pickle's robot had also been done to Julius's exoskeleton.

Ory rammed the churning robot into the miniature house again. And again, outside, something hit the real house with similar force.

Reed couldn't believe Shelly and her brothers were ignoring the sounds. How could they not hear them?

"You never said where you're going," Pickle said.

Another robot impact on the model house. Another *whump* outside.

Pickle didn't mention the mimicking sound.

Reed's legs gave out, and he dropped to the ground. He wasn't so eager to go outside anymore. No. He now wanted more than anything to stay inside . . . maybe forever.

He looked around. Were all the windows and doors locked?

What if they weren't?

No, of course they were. Mrs. Girard wouldn't forget

to lock up. She was as fanatical about safety as she was about keeping her children well fed.

"Reed?"

Reed looked at Pickle. "Oh, I forgot what I was thinking of."

"You forgot you wanted to leave a few seconds ago?" Pickle asked.

Reed nodded. "I think I ate too much. My brain is drowning in buffalo sauce."

Pickle came up with a partial smile. "Mom does make great chicken wings." He leaned forward. "Hey, I wonder if there are more. Or more of those popper things." He looked at his sister. "Hey, Shel, do you know if Mom put away any extra chicken wings or those popper things?"

Shelly looked up from her book. "Huh?"

"Chicken wings. Poppers."

"Oh, no. They're all gone," Shelly said. "And you can't be hungry already! How is it fair you get to eat so much and stay so skinny? My life would be paradisiacal if I could eat like you with no consequences."

Like paradise, Reed thought, in spite of himself.

Ory had stopped plowing the robot into the miniature house. Now he was circling the robot around the house at a dizzying speed.

"I can't help it if I'm hungry," Pickle told his sister.

"Well, you can't be hungry. Maybe you're just thirsty."

"I want a soda," Ory called out. It was the first thing he'd said since he'd returned to playing with Pickle's robot.

"Hey, that sounds good," Pickle said.

"We don't have any," Shelly said.

"Why?" Pickle asked.

"Remember? Mom read some article about the combination of carbonation and sugar? She discovered that our bodies process the mixture as if it was a poison in the system."

"Right. I do remember that." Pickle sighed. "We shouldn't let her read. All she seems to read are things that make our lives suck."

Reed, who by now had wound himself tighter than Pickle's grasp of basic math, blurted, "Your lives don't suck!"

Pickle, with an open mouth, turned to look at Reed.

"Sorry," Reed said. "Sorry."

Pickle said nothing, but Shelly put down her book and looked at Reed with one eyebrow raised.

Reed shrugged. "It's just that you're so lucky to live in this nice house and have a mother who always makes good food for you and loves you and . . ." He stopped because he felt like he was going to cry. And he did not want to do that.

It was the stress. He was making himself crazy with his panic.

The little robot started climbing up the side of

Shelly's miniature house. It looked like it had somehow grown suction cups on its legs. It scaled the side of the toy house as if it was a spider.

For a moment, Reed was mesmerized by the robot's functionality, but then he realized he was hearing something outside the Girards' house. Something new. Something majorly disturbing.

Something was crawling up the outside wall of the family room.

No, that couldn't be. Could it?

Reed tried to block out the sound of the little robot's clicks and drone. He listened hard beyond that. Wasn't that distant shuffling sound something on the house?

Yes. There. He could hear a sort of scrabbling, similar to what it sounded like when he once saw a raccoon climb up the side of his own house.

Maybe it was a raccoon out there now.

Maybe he was literally going insane and he was imagining all of this.

He had to be going insane. What he was hearing wasn't possible.

But then, why would he suddenly be going loopy? Was it guilt?

Was he such an unadulterated wuss that the *second* he did something a little gutsy, his brain lost its grip on reality? Was he going crazy just because he'd locked Julius into the exoskeleton?

"You're right," Pickle said.

Reed almost jumped out of his skin. "What?!"

Pickle cocked his head at Reed's peculiar behavior. "I said, you're right. We are lucky. It was illogical of me to have allowed that to escape my awareness. Perhaps my blood sugar is low. If I had a soda—"

"We don't have any," Shelly repeated.

"I want a soda," Ory said again.

He must not have wanted one badly because he was still playing with the robotic skeleton. He'd gotten it to climb up to the second-floor of the small house.

Reed jumped up and headed toward the stairs.

"Where are you going?" Pickle asked.

Reed stopped.

Good question. He didn't normally wander around the Girards' house as if he lived there. He'd been upstairs, of course, to both of the twins' bedrooms, and even in Ory's bedroom. But he'd only been in their rooms when they were in the rooms. What reason did he have to go upstairs now? What reason . . . besides his uncontrollable need to know if something was clutching onto the exterior walls of the house by the second-floor windows?

"Uh, sorry. I just thought of a book I need to borrow. I was going to go get it. I should have asked first."

Pickle studied Reed for a few seconds, and then he shrugged. "Sure. Go ahead. You don't need to ask. You're family."

This, for some reason, made Reed choke and cough,

THE BREAKING WHEEL

as if the words created an emotional hairball in his throat. But he knew it wasn't the words that were choking him. It was his guilt. No one in the Girard family would have done what he did to Julius, even if Julius was still just locked into his metal skeleton in the robotics classroom. They sure wouldn't have let Julius get tortured, possibly to death, by Pickle's remote. The second they even had an inkling that it might be happening, they would have gone to check.

What Reed lacked was initiative. Motivation. Impetus.

Aha! Nisus. An effort to attain a goal.

Reed shook his head. His brain was weird. Here he was in a total freak-out because he was pretty sure he'd tortured someone who was now climbing up the outside of the Girards' house in a giant robotic exoskeleton, and his brain was defining words of the day.

Maybe if Reed had had more *nisus* this evening, he could have saved Julius before Julius started crawling up the side of the house.

Stop it! Reed screamed in his head. *Julius is not on the side of the house!*

Oh, how Reed hoped he was out of his mind. He had a very, very, very bad feeling, though, that he was as sane as anyone. For some reason, he'd just become clairvoyant. Or was it omniscient?

Or maybe it was just observant and sensory-aware.

Because he could still hear something that was definitely not tree limbs crawling against the house.

Reed realized that Pickle had given him permission to go upstairs, and Reed was still standing here. What was wrong with him?

He shook himself and strode to the stairs. Then he ran up the stairs two at a time.

On the landing, Reed stopped and looked around. Now that he was here, what was he going to do?

If he looked out a window and actually saw what he was afraid he'd see, what was he going to do about it?

How could he get rid of Julius and his exosuit without his friends knowing? Heck, for that matter, how could he get rid of Julius, period?

Reed looked up and down the hall in complete indecision. What now?

Shelly's tidy white-and-green room was to the right. Shelly loved white and green. "The colors of purity and life," she once told Reed.

Pickle's cluttered, black-walled room was to the left. Ory's race-car motif bedroom was across from Pickle's room. A small pale yellow half bath was straight ahead of Reed.

Light suddenly shined through a window in the bathroom . . . from outside. Reed gulped.

He remembered that the Girards had motion-sensor lights in the backyard. One of them had just come on.

Reed stared at the window intently. But nothing

else happened. Except for the light, he didn't see anything. Nothing appeared in the window—no shadows, no movement.

He couldn't hear anything moving anymore, either. He strained to listen. Nothing.

Remembering he was supposed to be up here looking for a book, he figured he should head to Pickle's room and find something that he could come up with some plausible explanation for wanting. He ignored the prickly sensation on the back of his neck as he took a step in the dark hallway.

Images of Julius's bloody, maimed body jumped into the forefront of Reed's mind, and he had to swallow down a scream. *It's just my out-of-control imagination*, he thought.

Flipping a switch just inside the doorway of Pickle's room, Reed gratefully left the dark hall and entered his friend's domain. Stuffed with books, CDs, and scientific equipment, Pickle's room more resembled a laboratory than a bedroom. Only the twin bed with its constellations bedspread suggested the room belonged to a boy just into his teens. The rest of the space screamed, "Genius."

Reed crossed to Pickle's wall-to-wall bookshelf. He went to the section where he knew Pickle kept fiction. Pickle read more nonfiction than fiction, but he did have a selection of sci-fi books he claimed were as educational as many of his science books. Reed plucked one of those books from the shelf without looking at it.

After he had the book, he stepped over to the window and looked out past Pickle's gray curtains. Unfortunately, the light in the room gave him a view of little more than his own reflection. He hadn't thought that through, obviously. You don't try to see outside at night from a well-lit room.

But even with the reflection of the room in the way, Reed could see enough to tell that nothing was outside the window. Clutching the book he'd taken from the shelf, he turned toward the door. He spotted bloody tissues on Pickle's nightstand. Pickle's nose. Reed was supposed to remind him to ice his nose. He'd do that when he went back downstairs.

If he got to go back downstairs.

What if Julius, in his probably ruined state, was lurking outside one of the windows up here just waiting for Reed to appear so he could crash through the glass and get revenge? Why was Reed even up here? He should've been hiding far away from where he thought Julius and his exoskeleton was. Who went toward danger instead of away from it?

Someone who wasn't a hundred percent sure the danger was real.

Reed had to know whether his thoughts were right or crazy.

He made himself return to the hallway so he could continue his search for whatever was—or wasn't—out there.

It was still dark throughout the upstairs. And it was still silent.

Reed crept across the hall into Ory's bedroom. At the threshold, he tripped over something and caught himself by the doorjamb. His heart rate sped up. He'd heard a metallic *clink* when his foot made contact with whatever it was. What if it was an exoskeleton? He quickly turned on the light, almost afraid to see what was on the floor.

It was just a toy firetruck.

Reed exhaled.

He looked around Ory's chaotic mess. He couldn't remember seeing so many toy cars in one place, not even in a toy store.

Ory had one of those rugs with a race track on it. Toy cars were scattered all over the track, and beyond the race track rug onto the wall-to-wall carpet, too. Nothing unusual here. A bright red shade with a cartoon race car on it was pulled over Ory's single window. Reed couldn't bring himself to open that shade to look outside.

As he flipped the light switch and stood once again in the hall, it occurred to Reed that turning on lights hadn't been that smart. Not only did the interior lights impair his night vision, but the lights telegraphed where he was. If something was outside, it could be hiding when he turned on the lights.

Well, that was just dumb. Why would Julius be hiding?

If it was Julius outside.

If anything was outside.

Reed wasn't sure at this point that either possibility would bring him relief: either there was a broken and gory monster clinging onto the side of the house, or Reed was having a complete mental breakdown. Either way, he couldn't just stand here forever.

"Reed?" Shelly called from the bottom of the stairs.

Reed froze as if he'd been caught reading her diary or something. "Yeah?" His voice broke.

"We're going down to the corner to get sodas. Do you want to come with?"

"No, that's okay. You go ahead. I'll stay here if that's all right with you."

"Sure. Just don't go in Ory's room. You'll probably break a foot on one of his cars. I'm pretty sure he has some kind of vehicle assembly line in his room."

Shelly snorted when Ory protested in the background, "I do not! Wait. What's an assembly line?"

Reed smiled. For a second, he felt almost normal as he listened to Pickle, Shelly, and Ory head to the door.

"Oh, Reed?" Pickle called.

Reed went rigid again. He cleared his throat. "What?"

"Don't tell Mom where we went if she comes home early," Pickle yelled up the stairs.

"You're an idiot," Shelly told her brother. "You think she doesn't know everything we do?"

"She does?" Ory asked in an awed tone. *"Everything?"*

"Everything," Shelly said emphatically as the front door opened.

Reed listened to the stomps and shuffles of his friends leaving the house. The door slammed. He waited. He heard the lock slide into place, and he said a silent thank-you for the way Shelly had adopted her mother's safety consciousness.

At the same time, he became ultra aware that he was completely, one hundred percent alone in the Girards' house. If what he thought was outside was indeed outside, this could be bad for him. Really bad.

What if Julius had been waiting for an opportunity just like this?

But why? Why would Julius wait if he was a lacerated monster? Wouldn't he just want to kill anything in sight?

Wait. Now Reed's brain was really getting way out there. Just because Julius might have been mangled by the exoskeleton Reed had locked him into and Ory had inadvertently made it do things that tortured Julius with mind-crumbling pain didn't mean Julius had suddenly turned into a killer. He was still just a kid, maybe a horrible kid and maybe now even a badly injured kid, but just a kid.

But was he just a kid? Not really. Julius was a *really mean* kid.

Reed would never forget the day Julius first showed up in his school, in third grade. He wouldn't forget it because that's when his own torture started. Julius had been tormenting Reed for six years.

Julius seemed to thrive on humiliating other kids, and he seemed to get downright euphoric when he hurt them. For all Reed knew, Julius was already a killer. At the very least, he'd probably been murdering and dissecting squirrels for years.

So if Julius was now in unspeakable pain because of what Reed did, it made sense that he'd be even more homicidal now. Reed didn't know for sure, but he figured agony brought out the worst in a person.

The house creaked, and Reed leaped out of his pointless thoughts and back into the dark hall.

That sound was just the house creaking, wasn't it?

He listened for several minutes. When he didn't hear anything else, he crept down the hall to Shelly's room. He knew he wouldn't step on anything in here. She was obsessed with order. Going slowly, he felt his way through her room until he reached her window, which he knew overlooked the front of the house. Standing back from the edge of the window, he lifted the edge of her heavy green curtains and peeked outside.

Nothing was out there that shouldn't have been. Below the window, the porch roof stretched along the front of the house. By the street, the mailbox leaned a little to the left.

Two large cedar trees stretched their branches toward Shelly's window. One of the branches brushed against the side of the house. Although, as Reed had thought, it wasn't windy, there was a slight breeze, and the branch moved against the siding. Was this the sound Reed had heard earlier? Had he gotten himself all worked up for nothing?

He hoped so, but he didn't think he was worried about nothing. Scanning the night, he searched for any sign of movement. He saw none.

Stepping away from the window, Reed picked his way out of Shelly's room. In the hallway, he hesitated. Should he go into Mr. and Mrs. Girard's room?

He looked around.

As long as he didn't touch anything, why not? It wasn't like he was going to turn on the light and snoop around. He just wanted to look out their big window, which overlooked the backyard.

Reed crossed the hall and stepped into the master bedroom. A night-light near the master bath cast a dim glow throughout the room. It created creepy shadows, but at least it made maneuvering to the window easy. All he had to do was swivel a rocking chair away from the window and nudge aside the curtain. Then he was able to see . . .

Nothing unusual. Again, the yard looked the way it should. All was quiet.

Enough of this!

Reed dropped the curtain and strode from the room. He looked over the hall, then ran down the steps and returned to the family room.

The family room looked the way it had when he'd left it, minus the Girard siblings. Apparently, Pickle had a put a small log on the fire after Reed went upstairs, because the fire was flaring up behind the metal screen that protected the room from stray sparks. Pickle's book was on the end table next to his dad's easy chair. Shelly's book was lying on the sofa.

Reed sank to the cushy carpet.

He looked around. Where was the little robot?

He didn't see it. Did Ory take it with him?

Reed spotted the remote on the floor next to the sofa, but the robot wasn't in sight. Maybe Ory got it stuck under a piece of furniture.

Reed turned and looked at Shelly's miniature house. It really was an amazing thing. It seemed to be accurate in every little detail. All the furniture he could see on the front porch and inside the house through the open windows was exactly like the real furniture in the normal-size house. *What about the art and stuff?* he wondered.

He scooted over to examine the house more closely.

As he figured she would have, Shelly had re-created all the art and knickknacks inside the house. Anything in this real house was in the toy house. She'd even put pencil marks with dates on the wall just inside the kitchen doorway, the marks and dates that chronicled the Girard kids' growth over the years. And outside, one of the downspouts was bent just like the real one out front was. It got bent when Reed and Pickle were trying to learn how to throw a football. One of their errant tosses, though forceful, went badly askew and left a permanent indentation in the metal.

Reed shifted again so he could look at the miniature version of the room he sat in.

"Wow," he breathed.

There was a super-miniature house inside the miniature house! Talk about realism!

It shouldn't have surprised him that Shelly was that thorough with her model house. Shelly never did anything halfway. And if she couldn't do it well, she stopped doing it.

Reed remembered finger painting with Pickle and Shelly in kindergarten. The teacher had been wandering around telling everyone they were doing great, but when she got to Shelly, she didn't say anything.

"Aren't I doing great too?" Shelly asked.

"Of course, kiddo," the teacher said.

"You're lying," Shelly accused. "I can tell by your tone of voice." She stood up and put her hands on her hips, careful to avoid getting paint on her red pants.

Reed remembered watching the teacher think it over. She finally decided on truth. "Well, you aren't really getting the point of finger painting. It's to be free with the color and have fun. You're trying too hard, making everything too perfect."

"Fine," Shelly said. She reached up, grabbed her paper, and marched over to put her finger painting in the trash.

Reed grinned at the memory. Then he saw something silver and shiny glinting through the window at the back of the mini-model house's family room. He leaned forward and canted his head so he could see behind the mini-model house.

Aha. That's where the little robot went. It was inside the miniature house, behind the mini-miniature house.

Reed started to reach into the miniature house to rescue the robot. Before he could get a hand in through the front door, though, the little robotic skeleton raised up off the floor of the house.

Reed jumped, then started to shake his head at his edginess.

And that's when Julius sprang up from behind the model house.

Reed scrambled backward, screaming.

In his mind, he called what he was seeing Julius because his vivid imagination had prepared him to see the boy the way he looked now. But Julius didn't look a thing like Julius.

He was, in fact, exactly what Reed's mind had known Julius would be. Now nothing more than a fleshy octopus-like mass of pulpy limbs attached to a metal frame, Julius could no longer be called a boy. He couldn't be called human.

Reed wasn't even sure Julius was alive.

Yes, Julius moved, but Reed didn't know if that was Julius initiating the movement or if his corpse was just being controlled by the metal framework latched onto Julius like a loathsome external parasite.

Julius's face was slack, so there was no life there. It was slack because it looked like the bone structure of his forehead, cheeks, and jaw had been pulverized. His features were so distorted he resembled some kind of crudely sewn cloth version of himself. No longer framed by wavy blond hair because that hair was now sticky and stringy with congealed blood, Julius's face was like a repulsive doll's face, a doll much worse than Alexa's baby doll with the staring black eyes.

Julius's eyes were a thousand times more disconcerting than empty black ones. His eyes had rolled back in his head so all that was showing was the whites—the murky, cloudy whites. Those ghostly whites made him look like a sightless zombie.

But, like a zombie, Julius, alive or not, was moving. He was moving determinedly toward Reed.

Reed willed his legs to work, and he struggled to find his feet. Looking wildly around the room, he tried to decide on the best escape route.

The windows?

They had a complicated latching system. He wouldn't be able to get them open in time.

The doors?

Duh.

Reed ran toward the French doors. He knew they had a special lock, the kind that required keys on the outside or the inside, but the key was kept near the door, wasn't it? He scanned the area near the door. No key.

He realized he had no idea where the Girards kept the key. And he had no time to look for it.

Turning, Reed ran toward the entryway. The Julius-thing scuttled out from behind the miniature house and tumbled across the floor after him. Reed tore through the archway, rounding the corner and heading to the front door. Before he could get there, though, Julius sprang to the ceiling and skittered past Reed to block his way to the front door.

Reed didn't pause to consider his options. He just raced up the stairs.

Glancing over his shoulder, Reed watched in horror as Julius and his metal frame flailed crushed limbs grotesquely to catapult from the entry ceiling to the stairway wall. The Julius-thing scaled the stairway wall as Reed ran. Reed was barely able to stay ahead of his pursuer.

At the landing, Reed got a glimpse of Julius leaping to the ceiling again. Reed turned, aiming for Pickle's room. His plan, if he could call it that, was to use Pickle's scientific equipment as weapons to keep Julius at bay while Reed escaped out of Pickle's front-facing window. Like Shelly's, it was over the front porch roof, so Reed wouldn't have to drop two stories to the ground. Although at this point, he'd have dropped multiple stories if it meant getting away from Julius . . . or what was left of him.

Feeling something at the same time rubbery and sharp nick his shoulder as he tore into Pickle's room, Reed managed to get the light on as he entered. He grabbed the first piece of equipment he saw, a big and heavy microscope, almost too big and heavy for him to lift. But he managed.

Once he had the microscope in his firm grip, Reed turned and swung blindly out in front him. He was sure he'd connect with Julius because Julius was right on his heels.

But Julius wasn't there.

Reed looked around desperately. Where'd Julius go?

Reed looked up.

The Julius abomination dropped off the ceiling and landed on Reed before Reed could swing the microscope again. The impact knocked the microscope from Reed's hand. It tumbled across the room as Reed screamed and tried to squirm out from under the horrendous combination of hard and sharp metal and squishy, clammy destroyed body parts. At the same time, he tried to hold his breath because the Julius thing smelled dreadful. It smelled like blood, putrid flesh, and stale sweat. It was dripping on Reed, too. Julius's flesh and his no-longer-stylish clothing, perforated by puncture wounds caused by jutting cracked bones, was smeared with dried blood, and his body still seeped fresh blood, too.

Galvanized by his revulsion, Reed struck out at the metal and flesh that attempted to engulf him. He fought with all the strength he had and some he'd obviously gotten from someplace else.

At first, Reed thought he was going to be able to get away. Julius's hands didn't work right, and they couldn't grip Reed firmly. Reed managed to slither out from under Julius, and he stood, preparing to race around the bed to escape out the window.

But what Julius lacked in coordination and grip he made up for in speed. Reed made it halfway to the window, but then something caught his foot.

No, not *something*. Julius or his frame or both.

Reed looked back at the combination of metal and tissue that coiled around his ankle.

"Let me go!" Reed yelled.

Why did he waste his breath? Did he really think a shouted command would stop whatever Julius had become? It wouldn't have stopped human Julius. It sure wasn't going to stop this version of Julius.

Reed kicked out, and his foot slipped away just a little. But then Julius clamped down harder. How? How was Julius able to grip anything without working bones?

It didn't matter. Reed was just distracting himself with all these irrelevant thoughts. He was trying to put off the inevitable.

Reed wasn't going to get away from Julius, not even if he made it to the window. Julius was now powered by a robotic framework a mere human couldn't defeat, especially if that mere human was Reed. Plus, Julius now seemed to be supercharged by the monstrosity that he'd become. And that monstrosity had been born of the kind of emotions that propelled humans past their usual limitations. Emotions like pain and fear.

Emotions like rage.

Julius's rage was more powerful than Reed's guilt.

Reed didn't stand a chance.

But still, he tried. Kicking his feet as if power-swimming against the tide, Reed army-crawled across the rug. He willed himself away from what held on to him. He imagined himself going through Pickle's window and jumping to freedom.

Reed let out a banshee-like cry and yanked his foot from Julius's grasp. He staggered to his feet and turned toward the window.

Before Reed could take a step, though, Julius was on him again. This time, Julius fell fully onto Reed, and they both went down on Pickle's bed. Reed was pinned under Julius's hideous remains and the metal frame strapped to them.

Reed inhaled Julius's stench and gagged. Even as he gagged, he cried out, "Help!"

Whose help was he calling for? No one else was in the house.

Would the neighbors hear?

Reed's face was just inches from Julius's lifeless eyes and sagging mouth. Gagging again and whimpering, Reed turned his face away from the horror above him. He shut his eyes as if he could make his macabre attacker disappear by pretending it wasn't there.

His heart pounding so loud he could hear little else, Reed bucked and lurched, trying to free himself from the thing. But he wasn't strong enough. Even though Julius didn't seem to be gripping Reed in any way, his weight alone, along with that of the metal framework, was enough to pin Reed in place.

Reed was trapped.

Practically hyperventilating in shock and fright, Reed forced himself to open his eyes and look at Julius. When he did, he was sorry. He immediately closed his eyes again. He couldn't stand looking at the milky white, iris-less eyes staring down at him.

Or were they staring?

Reed didn't even know if Julius was conscious. How could he be with his bones crushed into smithereens? It was more likely Julius was dead and the movement of the thing he was strapped into was caused by some kind of short in the system. Maybe the interference of Pickle's remote had so badly fried the exoskeleton's systems that it was wildly functioning on its own now.

Something dripped into Reed's face. He had to open his eyes. It was worse not knowing what was happening above him.

Reed opened his eyes.

Okay, maybe not knowing wasn't worse.

Blood was pooling in the spongy mass of what used to be Julius's face. It looked like a misshapen sponge that had been used to clean up a massacre. And now it was dropping its warm, wet contents onto Reed's cheeks. The previously cream-colored scarf looped around Julius's neck was saturated, too. It hung down toward Reed like a dead animal in a slaughterhouse.

Mesmerized now by the whites of Julius's eyes bulging out from between long blond lashes, Reed couldn't turn away from the malformed thing above him. But he still struggled. Grunting, he shoved upward with all his might.

It did no good. It was like the weight of a hundred cars pinned him down.

"Please, please," Reed whispered. "I'm sorry. I'm really sorry. I didn't know this was going to happen to you. I just wanted you to be locked in overnight. I didn't want this to happen."

He knew there was no use in begging, but he couldn't help himself. He opened his mouth to say something else, but that's when the question of whether Julius had consciousness was answered. Julius shifted downward to press his heavy, seeping mass against Reed's mouth. Reed could no longer speak.

But he could hear.

In the distance, downstairs, the other kids were returning from their soda run. Reed could hear Pickle suggesting to Shelly that he could construct a better torture device than anything medieval people had come up with.

"I'm not sure that would be an accomplishment, Pickle," Shelly said.

Reed strained, grunting, desperate to get their attention.

Trying to yell, Reed could only make unintelligible groans.

Downstairs, Ory piped up. "Can I play with the remote again, Pickle?"

Julius shifted, and Reed allowed himself a moment of hope. Maybe he could get away.

Pouring every bit of life force he had into his muscles, he surged upward. He hoped to erupt like a volcano and get ejected away from Julius, toward freedom.

But he didn't erupt. Or rather, he did, but before he could get ejected away from the Julius cage that imprisoned him, Julius's mashed hands somehow grabbed hold of Reed's outstretched hands. Julius's formless legs somehow managed to wrap tightly around Reed's ankles.

Reed was now as linked to Julius as Julius was to his exoskeleton. And Reed knew what was going to happen next.

With the pressure of Julius's face wedged against Reed's throat, Reed couldn't make a sound that could be heard downstairs. He was facing his worst nightmare, and he couldn't scream.

Downstairs, Pickle responded to his brother's question. "Sure, Ory. Go nuts. We have all night!"

Ory grinned and knelt on the floor next to the miniature house. Usually interested only in cars and racing, Ory was surprised by how much fun this robot was. Maybe he could get his brother to build him other things. He'd never been able to get a robot to move this way before. It was super cool!

Pressing a button, Ory got the little robot to crawl out from behind the mini-miniature house. He carefully maneuvered the robot out of the miniature house, not wanting to get on his sister's bad side. One time, he ran the little skeleton into a wall. When he did, he heard something bump on the floor above his head.

He looked up, but he didn't hear anything else, so he continued carefully guiding the robot out of the house and onto the miniature porch. When he got it out, he did a little fist pump.

Happy with himself, Ory grinned wider and decided to see if he could get the robot to do even weirder things than it was doing before he got his soda. He began manipulating the remote so fast his fingers were just a big blur.

In response, the little robot shot off the toy house's porch and began spinning and thrashing. While Ory shouted in triumph, the little robotic skeleton began popping and snapping its metal limbs in all kinds of unnaturally delightful ways.

HE TOLD ME EVERYTHING

"I wish we were a nice family," Chris said. He and his parents and sister sat around the secondhand dinner table, eating hot dogs and canned baked beans and macaroni and cheese that had come from a box.

"What the heck is that supposed to mean?" Chris's dad said. He was still wearing his uniform from the garage with his name, DAVE, stitched in cursive letters over the shirt's breast pocket. "Do you think we're all a bunch of jerks or something? I mean, look at your mom—is this the face of somebody who isn't nice?"

Chris's mom flashed an exaggerated angelic smile and fluttered her mascara-painted eyelashes.

"And what about your little sister here—she's not nice?" Chris's dad pointed a forkful of macaroni and cheese in Emma's direction.

"I'm very nice," Emma said, pushing her glasses up on her freckled nose. She was in fourth grade and was,

Chris thought, bossy beyond her years. She gestured at her green uniform, complete with a sash full of badges. "I'm a Girl Scout and everything."

"See? It doesn't get nicer than that," Chris's dad said. "And everybody who knows me says I'm reasonably nice—the guys at the garage, my customers, my buddies I go bowling with. People tend to like me. Or at least, they generally don't run away when they see me approaching them." He reached for another hot dog—*a mistake, given his growing waistline*, Chris thought—and squirted it with an excessive amount of mustard. "So what do you mean when you say our family isn't nice?"

Chris felt like his father had misunderstood him. This was a regular occurrence. "No, you're all nice people," Chris said. "That wasn't what I meant. What I meant was"—Chris searched in vain for words that would express his thoughts without offending his family members—"I guess I don't know what I meant."

But really, Chris knew *exactly* what he had meant. His parents were decent people: good citizens who loved their kids and worked hard for their family and community. His little sister was annoying in the way younger siblings were, but he would never say she was a bad person. That being said, when he compared his family to the families of the smartest kids in school, they fell short.

Part of it was his parents' education, or lack thereof. His mom had started working as soon as she graduated high school and still had the same job at the utility board she had gotten when she was eighteen. After Chris's dad finished high school, he had gone to vocational school to learn how to work on cars. He had an excellent reputation as an auto mechanic, but that job didn't strike Chris as prestigious enough. His dad came home every day dirty and smelling like axle grease. In Chris's opinion, truly successful people didn't need to take a shower as soon as they got home from work.

When Chris went out with his parents, to a restaurant or a store or a school function, he always felt embarrassed. His mom was loud and flashy. She wore the brightest colors she could find with the reddest lipstick and the biggest, shiniest costume jewelry.

His dad, despite his daily after-work showers, always had grease under his fingernails, so he never looked quite clean. And then there was the matter of his weight. Chris's dad's belly protruded over his belt, and sometimes his shirt rode up such that the great shelf of his distended gut escaped and hung out for all to see. When he sat and his pants slipped down and his shirt rode up in the back, what he exposed was even worse.

Chris knew his parents were nice. He just wished they could look nice and act appropriately in public. The smartest kids at school had parents who always knew how to look and act. The dads wore jackets and ties or khakis and polos. The moms wore tasteful blouses and dress slacks and subtle, expensive jewelry and makeup. These parents were professionals: lawyers or engineers or medical doctors. They had careers that required years of schooling beyond high school. This was the kind of career Chris wanted.

The kinds of jobs that Chris's parents worked led to a deficiency in another area: money. They weren't poor, no. They owned their house, but it was a plain, dumpy house, barely big enough for a family of four, and the furniture was mostly hand-me-downs from Chris's grandparents. His mom and dad each had a car, but both of the vehicles were ancient and only kept running because of his dad's mechanical know-how. They had a creaky old shared family computer, and Chris's video game console was so tragically out of date he couldn't buy new games for it anymore. They only got basic cable. Honestly, who just had basic cable these days?

When Chris rode around town on the school bus, he always noticed the subdivisions that were full of fancy, two-story brick houses. He liked to fantasize about the families who lived in them: the doctor dads and lawyer moms and their high-achieving kids, all dressed in designer clothes, eating grilled salmon and steamed vegetables and salad for dinner and then lounging in rooms that looked like they were ready to be photographed for one of the home-and-garden magazines he always saw in the waiting room at the doctor's office. The parents probably played golf and tennis at the country club while their kids splashed around in the pool. There were never any worries about how to pay for the kids' college once they were old enough.

That's what Chris had meant by wishing they were a nice family. He wanted a nice life for them, with nice things, and a bright future for him and his sister. Surely it wasn't so wrong to want more out of life than scraping by every month just to pay the bills, then having to buy the off-brand items at the grocery store just to save a few cents.

"Emma, it's your turn to do the dishes tonight," Chris's mom said as they were finishing their meal.

"Okay, Mom," Emma said. It annoyed Chris how cooperative she always was. Didn't she ever get sick of doing the same chores over and over?

"Chris, I told Mrs. Thomas you'd help take out her trash tonight," Mom said, getting up from the table.

"After that, you can take Porkchop for his after-dinner walk."

Chris didn't want to do either of these tasks. Why were parents always exploiting kids for free labor? "Mom," he said, trying to keep his voice from rising to a whine, "I'm busy. Tomorrow's the first day of school, and I've got to get ready."

"Taking out Mrs. Thomas's trash and walking Porkchop will take thirty minutes, tops. That gives you plenty of time to get your stuff ready for school tomorrow."

He could tell from the tone of his mom's voice that she wasn't going to put up with any argument. "Okay, but I won't like it."

"I know you won't like it," his mom said. "It's part of my evil plan to oppress you." She did a fake laugh like a villain in a cartoon. "Come on, I'm trying to make you laugh here."

Emma, who was already clearing the table, laughed, but Chris wouldn't give his mother the satisfaction. With a theatrical sigh, he got up from the table and left by the back door to go to Mrs. Thomas's house.

Mrs. Thomas was old, so old that Chris's parents were always amazed that she still managed to live alone and take care of herself. She had been a high school English teacher for over forty years, teaching Chris's parents along with many generations of the town's high school students. Now, though, she had been retired and widowed for many years and lived in a small, boxy, book-cluttered house with just her cats for company. She cooked and did light housekeeping herself, but Chris's parents helped her out with anything that required heavy lifting.

Or, at least in the case of the garbage, they forced Chris to help her. The arrangement was that on the night before garbage day, Chris would come to Mrs. Thomas's house, empty all the trash cans in the house, and take the bags to the big garbage pail in her driveway, which he would then take to the side of the road so it would be ready for pickup the next morning.

Chris had once asked his dad if he could at least be paid for this weekly responsibility, but his dad had said, "Sometimes you don't do a job for money. You do it because it's the decent thing to do."

Chris had taken that as a no.

Chris knocked on Mrs. Thomas's door and prepared to wait. She moved slowly, and it always took her a long time to answer. When she finally came to the door, she was wearing the same yellow cardigan she wore year-round, even now when it was hot outside. She was a tiny, delicate, birdlike woman. Her glasses were thick, and her hair was thin and gray. "Hello, Christopher. It's so nice of you to come over and help me."

She was the only person who ever called him Christopher.

"Sure," Chris said. But really, it wasn't a matter of

being nice. It was more that he was still a kid and so when his parents made him do something, his only choice was to do it or suffer the consequences.

"Please come in," she said, holding the door open. "There's just one bag of trash that needs to go out. It's in the kitchen."

The house was dark and smelled musty. The walls were lined with full bookshelves, and every piece of furniture in the living room had at least one cat sleeping on it. He followed her into the kitchen.

"Could I interest you in some cookies before I put you to work?" Mrs. Thomas asked, gesturing to the cat-shaped cookie jar on the kitchen counter.

"No thank you. I just had dinner." Mrs. Thomas's cookies were the cheap kind they sold at the ninety-nine-cents store, and they were always stale. After taking her up on the cookie offer twice, he had learned to say no.

"Well, that's never stopped me from having a cookie or two," Mrs. Thomas said, smiling. "Your mother tells me you're starting high school tomorrow. That must be exciting for you."

"Yes, ma'am," Chris said, anxious for this conversation to end so he could get back to doing stuff that really mattered.

"She was bragging about what a good student you were and about how much you love to learn. You know, I taught at your high school for many years.

English literature. If you ever need any help with anything academic, just let me know. And if you ever want to borrow any of my books, you're always more than welcome to."

"Thanks, but I'm more of a science guy than a literature guy."

"Don't put yourself in a pigeonhole yet. You're too young," Mrs. Thomas said. "And there's absolutely no reason you can't be both a science guy and a literature guy. There are so many wonderful things in the world to learn."

Chris lifted the garbage bag, filled mostly with empty cat food tins, out of the trash can. "I'll take this out and then roll the big can out to the road, okay?"

Mrs. Thomas nodded. "Thank you, Christopher. You're such a great help to me."

Chris walked back toward his yard. He knew Mrs. Thomas was trying to be nice, but it was kind of sad that she thought she could help him with school stuff. She had gone to the little local college a bazillion years ago, then taught high school English until she retired. It wasn't like she was some great intellectual. Plus, she was so old she had probably forgotten what little she had known. He was sure she could teach him nothing.

Chris opened the gate to the fenced-in backyard, where Porkchop was wagging and waiting. As soon as Chris was inside, Porkchop jumped up on him and craned his neck so he could lick Chris's face.

"Get down, Porkchop! You're getting me all muddy!" Chris backed away from the dog's dirty paws and tried to dust off his pants.

Chris had wanted a dog, but Porkchop was not the dog he had wanted. Chris had wanted one of the smart, beautiful purebred dogs he had seen on dog shows on TV: a border collie or a Shetland sheepdog. But his dad had said they couldn't afford a purebred dog and that anyway, it was immoral to buy an expensive dog from a breeder when there were so many dogs in shelters that needed good homes.

And so one evening when Chris was in sixth grade, his dad had come home with Porkchop, a brown-and-tan, overgrown, snaggle-toothed shelter mutt who bore no resemblance to the elegant herding breeds Chris admired. It was immediately clear that Porkchop also lacked the intelligence to learn the tricks or agility skills Chris had dreamed of teaching a dog. Instead, Porkchop was a happy idiot whose favorite activities focused on his belly, either filling it or getting it rubbed.

"Ready for your walk?" Chris asked, without much enthusiasm.

Porkchop made up for Chris's lack of enthusiasm by wagging, barking, and running in small circles.

"If you won't sit, I can't put your leash on," Chris said. He couldn't believe how much time he was wasting carrying out his parents' orders.

He attached the leash to Porkchop's collar. "Once around the block, and that's all you get," he said.

Walking through the neighborhood was depressing. The houses were small and identical little boxes, which had originally been built for the workers in a steel mill that had shut down many years before Chris was born. The yards on which the houses sat were postage-stamp small. He was sure he was the only kid in the Science Club who lived in such a lousy neighborhood. He hoped he could keep where he lived a secret from the other kids, who, he was sure, all lived in the fancy neighborhoods on the west side of town that had names like Wellington Manor and Kensington Estates.

As promised, he took Porkchop around the block once, then brought him in the house and emptied out a can of dog food into his bowl. Porkchop happily gobbled it up.

Finally, with his chores all done, Chris could go to his room and start getting ready for the first day of high school. Not only did he need to get his backpack filled and organized, but he also had to decide what he was going to wear. His mom had taken him shopping the week before and bought him five shirts, three pairs of jeans, and some new sneakers. But they had gone to this awful big-box store because the prices there were affordable. What Chris had picked out looked okay, but he wished he could have real, name-brand clothes from one of the good stores in the mall. His mom said nobody could tell the difference, but he knew this was a lie she told to try to make him feel better.

Still, Chris was feeling hopeful. The first day of high school was a fresh start, a chance for him to prove himself. *A whole new ball game*, as his dad would say; the man never met a cliché he didn't like.

The thing that Chris was most excited about was joining Science Club. At West Valley High, Mr. Little's science classes and the club he supervised were legendary. Mr. Little's classroom was lit by plasma balls and lava lamps and strings of glowing bubble lights. He was famous for demonstrating spectacular experiments that involved fire or carefully controlled explosions, though he said he made sure his students didn't work on anything that would put them in actual danger. He was also famous for jump-starting student projects that produced extraordinary results and almost always won science fairs when West Valley competed with other schools.

Science Club was famous for bringing back numerous trophies for West Valley, and Science Club students had the reputation of being the school's highest achievers. On Freshman Orientation Day, when new students were given the opportunity to sign up for clubs, Chris had made a beeline for the Science Club table. It was the only club he signed up for. *Why waste your time on anything inferior*, Chris thought, *when you can be with the best?*

Chris was especially looking forward to this

weekend, which was the traditional lock-in that Mr. Little held every year for his students. The entire class would spend the night at the school, working on a secret project of Mr. Little's design. It had the reputation of being a life-changing experience, one that secured your status in Science Club and the school. Chris wanted his status to be the best of the best.

"Chris! Your friends are at the door!" Chris's mom called from the living room.

Josh and Kyle, Chris thought. He felt vaguely annoyed. He had a lot of preparation to do to ensure he made the right impression on his first day. He was in a serious mood, and Josh and Kyle were never serious about anything. "Be there in a minute!" he yelled back.

He finished loading his backpack with school supplies before he went to the door. At least he could get that done despite the interruption.

Josh and Kyle were waiting in the living room. Josh had let his hair grow out over the summer, and it hung in dark brown waves over his shoulders. Kyle had dyed a purple streak in his hair and was wearing a T-shirt for some band with a skull and crossbones on it. Chris was a little nervous about the fact that Josh and Kyle would also be starting at West Valley High tomorrow. They had been his friends since they were preschoolers, but he hoped they wouldn't hang all over him during school hours. They were nice guys, but he feared the image they projected wouldn't go over well with the Science

HE TOLD ME EVERYTHING

Club kids. He didn't want his old friends to hold him back from making new, higher-status friends.

"Hey," Josh said, pulling his hair back behind his ears, a habit he had picked up since letting it grow. "It's our last night of freedom."

"Yep," Kyle said. "Tomorrow they lock us back up and throw away the key until next summer."

"Actually, I'm kind of excited about going back to school," Chris said. "I mean, it's high school, you know?"

"Same thing with a different name," Josh said, sounding like he was bored already. "We were gonna ride our bikes over to the Dairy Bar, then go down to the lake. You wanna come?"

Of course you are, Chris thought. It was what they always did. But he supposed he might as well come along for old times' sake. Tomorrow, his life was going to change: It would be full of smart friends, science projects, and academic achievement. The bike rides and ice cream of childhood would just be a memory. "Sure, why not?"

He followed the boys outside and got his bike.

"Race you to the Dairy Bar!" Kyle yelled, like he always did.

They took off. Chris intentionally didn't pedal as fast as Josh and Kyle. He figured he might as well let them win. There were many achievements in his future, so maybe he should let one of them win the race to have some small sense of accomplishment. Soon he would be leaving them in the dust in other ways.

Josh won. Not that it mattered.

At the Dairy Bar, they each ordered their customary chocolate-vanilla swirl cones and sat down at one of the wooden picnic tables to eat them. Even though the ice cream was good, Chris could still imagine better treats he would have in the future once he had risen to the social status he aspired to. Then he would eat luxurious desserts he had only read about or seen on TV: crêpes suzette, molten chocolate lava cake, crème brûlée.

"I haven't seen you on the server much lately, Chris," Kyle said. In middle school they had liked to "meet up" online to play *Night Quest*, a popular multiplayer game, together.

"Yeah, I guess I've just had more important things on my mind lately," Chris said, licking his cone.

"Why? Is something wrong?" Josh asked. "Nobody in your family is sick or anything, are they?"

"No, nothing like that," Chris said. "I've just been thinking about, you know, the future."

"The future, like with robot overlords and flying cars?" Josh asked, grinning.

They were so incapable of being serious it was infuriating. "No," Chris said, "like my future. My goals. What I want out of life."

"That's some pretty heavy thinking for summer break," Kyle said. "At the beginning of the summer, I take my brain out, put it in a jar, put the jar on a shelf, and don't take it out again until school starts."

Josh laughed. "So that's what you'll be doing when you get home tonight? Putting your brain back in your head?"

"Nah, I'll probably wait till the morning. No need to start thinking any sooner than I have to."

Josh and Kyle were both laughing, but Chris couldn't muster a smile. How did he even end up being friends with these losers? He supposed it was just because Josh lived next door and Kyle lived across the street. They had been flung together because they were the same age and lived in the same place. If Chris had grown up in a nicer neighborhood, he would have ended up with a better class of friends.

After they finished their ice cream, they got back on their bikes to go to the lake.

What they called the lake was really just a large pond. Once they got there, they did the usual. They looked for flat stones to skip across the water. They tried to approach the Canada geese, then laughed when the geese hissed at them. They talked about video games and internet memes and nothing in particular.

Looking out at the "lake" that was really a pond, Chris thought of the word *stagnant*. That pond was going nowhere. It wasn't a river or even a little stream that flowed and went somewhere else, became a part of something bigger. Instead it just sat there, growing algae and gross bacteria, going nowhere and becoming nothing.

Unlike the pond, unlike Josh and Kyle, Chris had no intention of stagnating. He was going places.

Chris woke early on the first day of school. He took a shower, brushed his teeth aggressively, and applied a double coat of deodorant. He ran a little gel through his short, neatly cut sandy-brown hair to make sure it wasn't going anyplace. He put on the polo shirt and khakis he had set out the night before. He wished again that they were a better brand, but at least they were clean and new.

"Hey, there's my big freshman!" Mom said when he came into the kitchen. She assaulted him with a hug.

"Mom, stop," Chris said, squirming away from her and sitting down at the table. He poured himself a bowl of cornflakes and started slicing a banana over them.

Mom sat down across from him, holding a cup of coffee. She had already done her hair and makeup for work. As always, it was a little too much, in Chris's opinion. Her hair was dyed a shade of red that wasn't found in nature, and she was wearing a leopard-print top, black leggings, and leopard-print shoes. He wished she would aspire to simple elegance instead of cheap glamour.

"I know you get tired of me talking about how big you've gotten," she said. "But when you're a parent someday, you'll understand. You start out with this little, tiny baby with toes the size of corn kernels, and then it seems like no time passes till your baby's so tall you have to look up at him!"

Chris didn't comment, just crunched his cornflakes. What was there to say? He had grown. It was what kids did. It wasn't like it was some great achievement or anything.

"Anyway, I'm proud of you," his mom said. "Proud of your sister, too. It really seems like she should still be a baby, but you should've seen her this morning. She got herself all ready and walked to the bus stop. So independent." She smiled. There was a little smear of lipstick on her front tooth. "Say, I don't have to be at work till nine this morning. Do you want me to drive you in for your first day?"

Chris nearly choked on his cornflakes. He didn't want the Science Club kids at his new school to see his overly made-up mom pull in with her ten-year-old economy car that rattled and wheezed like somebody's great-grandpa. What kind of impression would that make? "No thanks, Mom. I'll just take the bus."

"What did I say? Independent." His mom reached over and ruffled his hair. Now he would have to comb it again.

On the school bus, Josh and Kyle were sitting next to each other. When Chris boarded, Josh said, "Hey,

Chris! Time to turn ourselves back in to the jailer, huh?"

Chris ignored him. There was an empty seat across the aisle from Josh and Kyle, but he ignored that, too, and found another empty seat farther back on the bus. It was better to be seen alone than to be seen in the wrong company. He looked around the bus, trying to figure out if any of the kids looked like they could be Science Club members.

West Valley High was much bigger and more crowded than Chris's old middle school. In the hallways, he had to concentrate to keep from running anyone over and not to be run over himself. It was hard to concentrate on navigating the hallway when his brain was consumed by one thought: Third period is Mr. Little's class. Third period is Mr. Little's class.

After what felt like an eternity and a half, third period arrived. Chris and his classmates crowded into the room at the end of the hall and beheld the bizarre wonders of Mr. Little's classroom. Chris took a seat and looked around. The walls were plastered with posters, some outlining the scientific method or showing cell structure, others displaying science-related puns and wordplay. One said, IN SCIENCE, MATTER MATTERS, and another, THINK LIKE A PROTON. STAY POSITIVE. The shelves that lined the room were filled with more scientific curiosities than Chris could take in at once. The one nearest him displayed a variety of glass jars filled

HE TOLD ME EVERYTHING

with clear fluid and different biological specimens. One jar held some poor creature's heart; another housed a fetal piglet with two perfectly formed heads. Yet another contained what looked disturbingly like a human brain.

Mr. Little stood before the lab table at the head of the classroom. He wore a white lab coat over a collared shirt and a brightly colored necktie printed with the design of a DNA helix. He was a small, energetic man—the literal incarnation of his last name—and he was smiling like the master of ceremonies in a particularly exciting show. His safety goggles, worn over his regular glasses, made his eyes look huge and insectoid.

"Come on in. Find a seat. Don't be shy," he said as students filtered into the classroom. "I promise there will be no major explosions or dismemberments. At least not on the first day." He flashed a naughty grin.

Chris didn't know everything he would be learning in the class, but he already knew one thing: he had never met a teacher like Mr. Little.

"All right, let's go ahead and get started," Mr. Little said, though the tittering among the students didn't die down. Chris expected Mr. Little to raise his voice, take out his roll book, and start taking attendance, but instead he poured some kind of clear solution into a glass container he held over a Bunsen burner. Within seconds, a huge fireball appeared, its flames falling just short of licking the ceiling, then disappeared instantaneously.

Everybody in the classroom gasped.

"I thought that would get your attention," Mr. Little said, grinning. "But I promise, you ain't seen nothin' yet!" He looked around the room. "This is science! And it is not for the faint of heart or the cowardly. It's not about just reading a textbook and answering questions correctly. It's about innovative thinking. It's about getting your hands dirty. It's about experimenting, with all that the word *experiment* implies. Sometimes we succeed, and sometimes we fail, but either way, we learn. In this class, I may ask you to do some stuff that sounds kind of crazy, but I promise that if you bear with me and follow my advice, by the time you're done with this course, you'll be thinking, talking, walking, and quacking like a scientist." He looked around the room. "Now who's ready to learn some cool stuff?"

Everybody clapped, hooted, or cheered. Chris already felt like he was a member of an exclusive club.

"Now, before we get to the fun stuff, we have to jump through a few bureaucratic hoops," Mr. Little said, "the first being this lab safety contract, which you and your parents must read and sign, saying that you will not intentionally blow up the school or another classmate."

"Aw, where's the fun in that?" a kid in the front row asked, and everybody laughed.

"Oh, it's always good fun until you have to scrub somebody's viscera off the walls," Mr. Little said. "I do hate it when students leave a mess."

More laughter.

The boy sitting in front of Chris raised his hand and asked, "Are you going to talk about the lock-in?"

"Yes," Mr. Little said. "There will be a meeting in this room right after school today for everybody who's interested in coming to the lock-in this weekend. I strongly suggest that you all come both for the sake of your grades"—he mouthed the words *extra credit*—"and for the sake of science!"

Once class was dismissed, the boy in front of Chris turned around. "I haven't seen you around before. Are you a freshman?" His brown eyes were intense and intelligent.

"Yes," Chris said. "How about you?"

"Sophomore," the boy said. "Sanjeet Patel. Everybody calls me San."

"Chris Watson." San radiated not only intelligence but confidence. Chris suddenly, desperately, wanted this kid to like him.

"Are you doing Science Club?" San asked as they gathered their belongings.

"Sure. It's practically all I've thought about since I knew I was coming to West Valley."

San smiled. "Once you're in, it'll still be all you think about. Do you have lunch next period?"

Chris nodded, hoping for a lunch invitation. This conversation seemed to be going well.

"So do I and a lot of Science Club people. Why don't

you sit with us and let everybody get a look at you and see what they think?"

"That would be great. Thanks." Chris was happy to be included, even if it was seemingly on a trial basis.

In the cafeteria, he sat with San and two other kids—a tall, lanky, red-haired boy who introduced himself as Malcolm, and Brooke, a petite Black girl with springy, dark curls.

"Chris is in Mr. Little's third-period class with me," San explained by way of introduction as they settled down to eat their lunches. Chris was the only one of them eating the lunch the cafeteria provided. The others all had packed lunches with fresh fruit and raw vegetables and sandwiches on whole wheat bread. Chris made a mental note to tell his mom that he wanted to start bringing his lunch. He would also have to be specific about what kind of foods to buy and pack. He couldn't let these kids see him eating peanut butter and jelly on soggy white bread.

"Well, you must be reasonably intelligent, then," Malcolm said, looking Chris over. "Mr. Little only lets a handful of freshmen into his level-two classes."

Brooke smiled. "Yeah, the freshmen who don't make the cut have to take Mrs. Harris's earth science class."

"I know, right?" Chris said. Josh and Kyle were in Mrs. Harris's class.

"Oh, come on, guys. They do lots of really challenging experiments," Malcolm said, "like mixing vinegar and baking soda to make a volcano." His voice dripped with sarcasm.

"You're terrible," Brooke said, but they all laughed.

"They also collect fall leaves and glue them to construction paper," Malcolm added. "Though it's too hard an assignment for most of them."

Chris laughed some more along with his—he hoped—soon-to-be friends.

San could hardly contain himself. "And their final exam," he said, laughing so hard he almost couldn't speak, "is to try to find the school cafeteria."

"Many fail, of course," Malcolm said, snickering.

Chris couldn't remember the last time he had laughed so hard. Of course, he felt a little bad because when he laughed about the stupidity of Mrs. Harris's students, he was also laughing at Josh and Kyle, who had been his friends since he was old enough to walk and talk.

But he knew if he was going to reach his goals, he couldn't be sentimental. It was time to move up to a better class of friends.

As soon as the dismissal bell rang, Chris hurried to Mr. Little's classroom. He couldn't wait to hear about the lock-in. Other students must have felt the same way because when he got there, the room was nearly full and abuzz with chatter. He found an empty seat near San.

"I wonder what Mr. Little has cooked up this year," San said to Chris.

Chris smiled. "I don't know. I hope it's cool."

"Oh, it will be," San answered, as though Chris's statement implied some kind of doubt in Mr. Little's abilities. "Until you've experienced it, you can't possibly understand. It will be life-changing."

Chris nodded. He guessed he didn't understand, but he was looking forward to learning. And a life-changing experience was exactly what he needed.

"Hey," San said, "Malcolm and Brooke and I have a study group that meets at Cool Beans Coffee on Wednesdays after school. You should come."

"Are you sure? Are Malcolm and Brooke okay with it?" Chris asked. He didn't want to appear pushy, like he was trying to force his way into their friend group.

"Yeah, they suggested it," San said. "They like you."

Chris smiled. He could feel his life changing already.

The room fell silent when Mr. Little entered. He walked down an aisle of the classroom like a celebrity walking the red carpet. When he stopped and stood before them, he said, "Greetings, my sweet little guinea pigs! Are you ready to hear what kind of experience I have planned for this weekend?"

The students clapped and hooted. Chris wasn't used to seeing such displays of enthusiasm in a classroom. It was a refreshing change.

"First of all," Mr. Little said, starting to pace, "science requires sacrifice. If you're not willing to make a sacrifice, to give up a part of yourself for the sake of science, then don't bother coming in on Friday because this lock-in isn't for you. Stay home and do whatever it is you do on your little electronic devices or go play a sport or whatever. Only come here if you are willing to make a sacrifice and experience a transformation."

Transformation. Chris felt like that was the word he had been looking for to describe what he was seeking. He wanted to transform his life, to transform himself, into something different, better, more worthy.

"In the past, some of our Science Club lock-ins have been group activities. This activity is one you will do alone. In fact, each of you will have a cubicle sequestering you from the other students and from me as well. Each of you will be issued your own Freddy Fazbear Mad Scientist Kit to work with. In this kit, you will find a solution called Faz-Goo. You will put the required amount of Faz-Goo in the provided petri dish." He smiled. "Then comes time for the sacrifice. With the pliers I will provide, you will pull one of your teeth—"

A gasp rose from the crowd. Chris heard himself gasp, too. *One of their teeth?* Surely he hadn't heard Mr. Little correctly.

"Excuse me, Mr. Little, could you repeat that part?" one student asked in a nervous-sounding voice.

"Teeth!" Mr. Little yelled. "You will pull one of

your teeth! It might hurt a little, but trust me . . . it will be worth it in the end. Now, are you scientists, or are you a bunch of sniveling babies?"

"Scientists!" most students yelled back.

"Good." Mr. Little resumed his pacing. "So you will pull one of your teeth, as I said, and you will place it in the Faz-Goo. Then you'll do what scientists spend a great deal of their time doing. You will wait. You will be provided with a cot to nap on while the process unfolds."

"And what process is that?" one student asked.

"Well, what fun would it be if I told you that? All I'll say is that it is the process of discovery!" Mr. Little's eyes were wild with excitement. "You will know when you're done because the results will speak for themselves. Literally. Then you will dispose of your creation in a biohazard bag and leave, a changed person. And not just dentally, but mentally!" He cackled at his own joke, and many students joined in on the laughter.

"There is a rumor," Dr. Little said, "that not participating in the lock-in hurts your performance in my classes. This is not exactly true. If you do not participate in the lock-in but you successfully complete all course requirements, you will still pass my class, possibly with an above-average grade. However, over the years I have found that the students who do participate in the lock-in demonstrate a level of commitment that allows them not just to pass, but to *excel*. And the fact that the lock-in is worth five hundred points of extra credit doesn't hurt, either." He grabbed a stack of papers off his desk. "Now for those of you who are up for this challenge, I will now distribute the required parental permission sheets that allow you to participate in the lock-in. But please, make sure you don't say anything to your parents about the required tooth extraction. I don't want to be on the receiving end of any dental bills. Also, as a community of scientists, we must keep our secrets."

Chris felt excited but also scared. He wouldn't let his fear stop him, though. You didn't transform yourself by playing it safe. You had to take risks, try new things.

When Dr. Little offered him a permission sheet, he grabbed it.

There was only one part of the lock-in that Chris dreaded. The more he had thought about it, the more nervous he became at the prospect of pulling out one of his own teeth. Chris had always been squeamish about dental matters. When he was little and had a loose baby tooth, he would procrastinate pulling it until the tooth hung by the smallest of threads. Sometimes, if he was lucky, the tooth would just come out without him even having to touch it. He lost one in an apple once, another in an ear of corn. Another time, when he had one tooth that he had been letting hang on for a number of weeks, his dad asked to see it, then yanked it out without warning. Chris had been mad at him for days.

Then there was the matter of dental visits. Even if it was just an exam and a cleaning, Chris was consumed with anxiety for weeks before. His mother told him she loathed his trips to the dentist as much as he did because she was the one who had to get him there and put up with his moaning and groaning before, during, and after.

Chris lay awake all night thinking. The lock-in was two nights away. If he could just figure out a way to participate in the experiment without having to pull his own tooth . . .

"Chris! Your friends are at the door!" his mom called.

Again? Chris thought. It showed how much less serious Josh and Kyle were that they'd show up and want to hang out on a school night. "Tell them I have homework!" Chris yelled.

"Come tell them yourself!" his mom yelled back.

Chris rolled his eyes but got up from the bed. He went to the door to see Josh and Kyle. "Hey," he said, "I can't hang out tonight. I've got homework."

"We just stopped by for a sec," Josh said. "Kyle's mom is going to drive us to the mall on Friday. We're going to eat at the food court and see the new *Revengers* movie. We wondered if you wanted to come."

It was kind of them to ask, but their pastimes seemed so childish now. "Thanks, guys. I'd love to, but I've got the Science Club lock-in that night."

"Oh, you're doing that?" Kyle said, sounding incredulous. "It seems kind of sad to spend most of a weekend in school."

"Well, I think it's exciting," Chris said.

Kyle and Josh exchanged a look.

"Just don't get too deep into the Science Club stuff, okay?" Josh said. "Some people in Mrs. Harris's class were talking about it yesterday. They say it's weird, like a cult or something."

Chris couldn't help but be offended. Josh and Kyle might not be cut out for Science Club themselves, but they could at least show it the proper respect. "Well, people in Science Club talk about the people in Mrs. Harris's class, too," Chris said.

"Yeah," Kyle said. "They say we're dumb."

"Because they're snobs," Josh added.

Kyle gave Chris a strange look. "You're not turning into a snob, are you, Chris?"

"No, of course not," Chris said. He hated that word, *snob*. It was what underachievers called high achievers to try to make them feel better about themselves. Well, he refused to take the bait.

"Do you think Josh and me are dumb?" Kyle asked.

Chris cringed a little. *It's "Josh and I,"* he thought reflexively. *And you're not dumb; you just lack maturity and ambition*. But he figured it would be a bad idea to say either of those things out loud.

"No, of course not," Chris said again. "Look, guys, I've got to get back to my homework. Maybe we can do something next Friday, okay?"

They said "Sure" and "Okay," but Chris could feel the distance between him and his old friends growing. It was a painful transition, but it was probably for the best.

"Bye, guys," Chris said and shut the door.

In the living room, Chris's mom was leaning over Emma, who was sitting on the couch.

"Count to three out loud before you do it, okay?" Emma said.

"Before you do what?" Chris asked.

His mom looked over at him. "Emma's got a loose tooth. I'm going to pull it for her."

Chris felt his stomach lurch. "Well, don't do it while I'm in here! You know that stuff grosses me out." Why couldn't his family tend to distasteful matters in private instead of in the middle of the living room? It was just a sign of how unrefined they were.

Mom laughed. "Wait till you're a parent. None of the stuff that grossed you out as a kid will bother you anymore."

Chris shook his head. "I don't know about that. If I have a kid, he'll definitely have to pull his own loose teeth." Chris fled the scene of the tooth extraction and went back to his room. As soon as he was alone, his thoughts turned to the Science Club lock-in. The idea hit him like a jolt of electricity.

Loose tooth. Of course! That's the answer.

Chris had walked past Cool Beans Coffee probably thousands of times, but he had never gone inside. For some reason, it just hadn't felt like it was for him. It was too sophisticated and adult, full of professionally dressed grown-ups sitting with their laptops and cardboard cups.

But today that was going to change. Chris was going inside.

He swung the door open and was immediately greeted by the dark, toasty smell of coffee. Paintings by local artists hung from the café's redbrick walls. Chris had to tell himself not to be nervous, that from now on this was the kind of place where he belonged.

"Hi, Chris!" San waved at him from where he and Malcolm and Brooke were sitting, their table strewn with open textbooks, notebooks, and coffee cups. "Get a drink and join us."

"Great! I will!" Chris called back. He studied the menu board over the counter. It was more confusing than anything he had ever studied in a class. There were mochas and frappes and cappuccinos and lattes. There were single shots and double shots and decaf and half-caff. Chris had never taken so much as a sip of coffee before, and he had no idea what any of these words meant.

The pretty young woman at the counter said, "May I help you?"

"Sure, I'm just not a very experienced coffee drinker, so I don't really know what I want."

She smiled. "How about if I just make you something I think you'll like?"

Chris was relieved to have the responsibility out of his hands. "Sure."

"Do you like chocolate?"

"Of course. I'm not stupid." *What kind of weirdo didn't like chocolate?* Chris thought.

She smiled again. "Let's try an iced mocha, then. Give me just a couple of minutes."

She turned her back on him and poured some different syrups in a machine. Chris couldn't decide if her actions looked more like chemistry or wizardry. Shortly after, she returned with a huge, clear plastic cup filled with what appeared to be rich chocolate milk topped with whipped cream and chocolate shavings. It looked like the world's fanciest milkshake.

The price she quoted was two dollars more than he expected, and he hoped his new friends didn't see him having to dig through his pockets and his backpack for change.

He took his expensive beverage and joined San, Malcolm, and Brooke at their table. They were all drinking hot coffee from paper cups, and compared to theirs, his milkshake-like drink looked childish. He had to admit it was delicious, though.

"So it looks like we're going to France this winter break . . . *again*," Malcolm was saying. "I really wanted to do Italy, but my mom can't pass up the shopping in Paris. I'm going to be bored to tears."

"I think we're doing a Caribbean cruise this year. I guess it'll be okay," San said. He turned to Chris. "We were just talking about family vacations and how we never get any say in where we go."

"Same here," Chris said. He hoped they didn't ask him about where his family had gone on vacation. Chris's family vacations were always the same. His parents took a week off in the middle of the summer, and they rented a cabin at a state park that was a couple of hours away. They spent the week fishing, swimming, hiking, and cooking out. It was always hot and buggy. For the most part, they had fun, but Chris knew it was a poor people's vacation.

"Ooh, that looks good," Brooke said, nodding toward his drink. "Is that a mocha?"

"Yes," said Chris. He was going to have to study up on coffee lingo. His parents drank coffee, but just the kind you bought at the grocery store and made at home.

"Mine is, too," she said. "Just hot instead of iced."

Chris felt less self-conscious about his drink now. *You need to loosen up around your new friends*, he ordered himself. They had invited him to join them. They wanted him here. It was time for him to start acting like he belonged.

"So what kind of results do you think the experiment at the lock-in will produce?" San asked, looking around the table.

"Well, clearly we'll be growing some kind of tissue," Malcolm said, sipping his coffee. "I just don't know what it will do."

"It'll do something, though, that's for sure," Brooke said. "Hopefully nobody will end up in the emergency room like last year."

Chris almost choked on his coffee. "Wait, what?"

Brooke laughed. "Some kid didn't follow the instructions right and ended up having to have a couple of fingers reattached. It was his own fault, though. He ended up transferring to Mrs. Harris's science class, where he was less likely to maim himself."

"The experiments are always perfectly safe if you know what you're doing, but that kid clearly didn't," Malcolm said. "Speaking of knowing what we're doing, if we're calling ourselves a study group, we'd better get down to studying."

Chris was usually already home when his mom came in from work, but today she beat him there.

"There you are," she said when he came in. "I signed your permission slip for the school thing. I was worried when I didn't see you here. I was just about to call and check on you." She was sitting on the couch with a glass of iced tea, her bare feet propped up on the coffee table. She didn't move, but extended a hand with the paper.

"I've joined a study group that meets after school," Chris said, pocketing the slip.

His mom laughed. "If some other kid told me that, I might think he was lying so he could run around after school doing who knows what. But I believe you."

"I know I'm a nerd," Chris said, sitting beside his mom on the couch.

"I'm *proud* you're a nerd," she said, smiling.

"I was wondering," Chris said, "might it be possible for me to have a small increase in my allowance?"

Mom took her feet off the coffee table and sat up straighter. "How much are we talking?"

Chris tried to calculate a figure that wasn't too outrageous but still would cover the price of expensive coffee drinks at study group meetings. "Ten dollars?"

Mom furrowed her brow and made a low whistling sound. "And what do you need ten more dollars a week for?"

"It's this study group, actually. We meet at Cool Beans downtown, and I need money for coffee."

"Gotten hooked on the stuff already?" his mom said, shaking her head. "Listen, kid, those froufrou coffee drinks are real money suckers. One gal I work with used to buy one every day, and when she quit the stuff, she was amazed how much money she saved."

The fact that she was lecturing him was not promising.

"Why can't you guys study at the library?" his mom asked. "The library is free."

Chris felt a wave of annoyance sweep over him. "Mom, I didn't start the study group; I just joined it."

"Well, maybe you could suggest meeting in the library. I'm sure it would save everybody a lot of money."

Chris rolled his eyes. "If I suggest that, they'll think I'm poor. Which I am, compared to them."

His mom sighed. "If they're your friends, they don't care how much money you have, and you shouldn't care how much they have, either."

"Mom," Chris said, on the verge of losing his temper, "that's not the way the world works."

She sighed. "I know it's not. I wish it was, though." She looked at Chris with a sad little smile. "Okay, I can give you *five* more bucks a week, but that's all. I'm glad you're making friends who take school seriously. Study hard so you can get rich and support me in my old age."

"Thanks, Mom," Chris said. This time, he didn't object when she gave him a hug.

Chris was buzzing with excitement as he walked to Mr. Little's classroom after school on Friday. He knew the lock-in was going to be a transformative experience, probably the most important experience in his life to date. He hoped he could complete the experiment to

Mr. Little's satisfaction and gain his approval as well as the approval of the other Science Club members.

Chris wasn't the only student who was excited. As he entered the classroom, he could feel the high level of energy. It felt electric. Everybody was talking and laughing. Some people stood and paced instead of sitting at their desks, too restless to sit still. Chris took his usual seat behind San.

San turned around and grinned at him. "Your first lock-in. This is a big day for you, right?"

"Yeah," Chris said, smiling back.

"It is for me, too," San said. "But it's even bigger for you because it's your first time. After tonight, you'll be a full-fledged member of Science Club!"

"All eyes on me, all mouths closed," Mr. Little called from the head of the classroom. "I know you're excited—heck, I'm excited, too!—but there are some very important directions you have to follow exactly, or the experiment won't work." He pushed his glasses up on his nose. "I have also taken the liberty of ordering some pizzas, which should be here shortly."

Cheers rose from all over the classroom.

"It's going to be a long night, and you should never conduct scientific research on an empty stomach. But while we wait for sustenance, allow me to explain more specifically what you'll be doing tonight. As you can see, I have set up private cubicles for each of you in the lab. In your cubicle you will find a long table and a cot for napping. On the table, you will find a Freddy Fazbear Mad Scientist Kit."

There were a few chuckles in the class, and one kid said, "But isn't that kit just a toy?"

"It is most definitely *not* a toy," Mr. Little replied, his voice turning stern suddenly, "and if you treat it as one, it will be at your own peril." He held up the kit for everyone to see and then opened it. "In the kit you will find a container of Faz-Goo and a petri dish, like this." He held up a vial of pink glop and a small dish. "You will empty the Faz-Goo into the petri dish. Then comes the sacrifice."

"The tooth," Chris half whispered.

"Yes, the tooth!" Mr. Little said, grinning wildly. "You will use the pliers"—he held up a pair of pliers—"to extract the tooth of your choice. I would advise one near the back. When your wisdom teeth come in, you won't have to worry about crowding."

Chris heard a sharp intake of breath from someone behind him. All of a sudden, his stomach felt queasy at the thought of the tooth extraction. He was glad he had figured out a way around it.

"If you can't handle this part of the experiment, now is the time to leave." Mr. Little looked around the classroom. "It's time to separate the real scientists from the wannabes."

Chris looked around the room. Some kids looked scared, but none of them moved.

"Good," Mr. Little said, nodding in approval. "I like my students to be fully committed. After you have extracted the tooth, you will place it in the petri dish of Faz-Goo. And that," he said, rubbing his hands together, "is when things start to get interesting. You see, the Faz-Goo will not only make the tooth stay alive . . . it will make the tooth believe it is still a part of you."

"A tooth can *believe* something?" Brooke asked.

"Well, it can feel that it's still inside your mouth," Mr. Little said. "The Faz-Goo is very powerful. When you touch it, it creates a tendril—a connection—that slowly pulls red blood cells from your body. The blood cells feed the Faz-Goo and fuel the experiment. And here's the amazing part: Over the course of several hours, nourished by just a few of your red blood cells, the tooth will grow gums, will form a full mouth, and that mouth will open up and tell you something that I promise, no matter how old you live to be, you will never forget."

Chris looked around at his classmates, all of whom were wearing an identical look of disbelief.

"You'll see," Mr. Little said, looking around at all the stunned faces. "It will be amazing. Once the mouth has told you what you need to know, it will die. I have provided a biohazard bag in each cubicle. You will dispose of the mouth and the Faz-Goo in the bag. After you have brought me the bag so I can dispose of it correctly, you are free to go." Mr. Little looked toward the classroom door and smiled. "But first, pizza!" He waved for the pizza delivery guy to come in. "You have thirty minutes to eat, drink, and socialize," Mr. Little said. "But after that, it's time to get to work!"

Chris grabbed a couple of cheese slices and a paper cup of soda and sat down with San, Brooke, and Malcolm.

"I guess this will be the last pizza I chew with my left back molar," Malcolm said, but he sounded more amused than scared.

"I'm a little worried pulling one of my teeth will mess up my orthodontia," Brooke, who had a mouthful of braces, said.

"Yeah, your orthodontist is going to be mad," San said. "Will your parents be mad, too, when they find out?"

Brooke shrugged. "Not if I tell them it was a Science Club assignment. They'd let me saw off my own arm if they thought it would improve my chances of getting into a good college."

"My parents would, too," Malcolm said, and they all laughed. "They'd let me saw off both arms if it would get me into the Ivy League."

"My mom will definitely be mad," San said.

Brooke laughed. "Oh, she will, won't she? I forgot!"

"Forgot what?" Chris said.

Brooke laughed some more but managed to get out, "San's mom is a dentist!"

After they laughed some more, Malcolm said, "That reminds me, Chris. I don't believe you said what your parents do for a living."

Chris felt a flutter of panic in his belly. He couldn't possibly tell them that his mom was a cashier where people paid their electric bills and that his dad fixed people's cars. "Um . . . my mom is an electrical engineer, and my dad is a mechanical engineer."

"Wow, two engineers for parents!" San said. "You must be really good at math."

Chris nodded. This part, at least, was true.

"Okay," Mr. Little called. "Time to get to work, scientists!"

Chris was glad that he hadn't revealed to San, Malcolm, and Brooke that he was going to perform the experiment without having to pull his own tooth. He couldn't let anybody know that he had figured out a way to game the system.

Chris entered his cubicle and filled the petri dish with Faz-Goo as instructed. Within a couple of minutes, he could hear grunts and groans as the students in the other cubicles labored to pull out their teeth. In the cubicle nearest him, he heard a scream, followed by a sickening popping sound as the tooth released from its root.

Chris figured that for the sake of realism, he should grunt and groan a little, too. He faked it for a few minutes, very believably, he thought, and then he reached into his pocket and pulled out his ace in the hole.

The sight of his mom about to pull his sister's tooth the other night had made him remember that when he was little, he had declined money from the Tooth Fairy in order to keep all his old baby teeth. He didn't know why he hadn't been willing to let them go, especially for cash, which was hard to come by in his family. He had been a weird little kid. But now that weirdness was paying off.

Chris submerged his old baby tooth in the Faz-Goo. When he touched the goo, he thought he felt a slight sucking sensation in his fingertips. He pulled his hand away, but a tendril of pink slime connected his index finger to the petri dish with his tooth in it. The tendril was stretchy, like mozzarella cheese when you lift the first slice from a hot pizza.

Now there was nothing to do but wait for the tooth to get what it needed from him. He lay down on the cot, making sure not to break the tendril that connected his finger and the Faz-Goo.

Chris closed his eyes and let himself doze. Soon he was dreaming of future successes. He saw himself as though he were a character in a movie, opening the letter granting him a full scholarship to an Ivy League university. He saw himself doing research in a lab at the university. The lab was bright and clean and filled with the most cutting-edge equipment. A distinguished professor in a white lab coat stood behind him and looked over his shoulder, smiling at the good work he was doing. Chris saw himself in a black cap and gown, walking across a stage. The university professor handed Chris his diploma, and Chris smiled to have his picture taken.

But when Chris smiled, it was immediately clear that something was wrong. Blood dripped from his lower lip down his chin. His mouth was a black cavern framed by a bloody mess of gums.

Somebody had pulled all of Chris's teeth.

Chris startled awake. He was disoriented at first, waking up on a narrow cot in a cubicle, but then he saw the tendril strung between his finger and the petri dish and remembered where he was and why.

Sitting up, Chris heard movement and whispering coming from the other cubicles. Could the whispering be coming from the mouth that this experiment was supposed to create? Chris pressed his ear to the partition in hopes of making out what was being said, but no words were discernable. From where he was, the whispering just sounded like the soft whooshing of wind through trees.

But then he heard the voice of the student in the cubicle next to his.

"Wow," she said, her voice filled with awe. "Wow."

There was a rattle of plastic, which could have been the biohazard bag, then the sound of footsteps. Chris pushed one of his cubicle's partitions open just a crack so he could watch the student leave.

It was Brooke, but the look on her face was different

than her usual smart, collected expression. Somehow her features seemed softer, more open. Her eyes were wide and full of wonder. She walked up to Mr. Little and handed him the biohazard bag.

Brooke rested her hand on Mr. Little's forearm and looked him in the eyes. "She told me everything," Brooke said.

Mr. Little smiled. "Good. Nice work, Brooke. You're free to go."

Brooke smiled back at Mr. Little and wandered toward the door.

Chris was just about to close the small opening in the partition when he saw another student, a tall, dark-haired boy he hadn't met yet, emerge from a cubicle across the classroom. Just like Brooke, he wore an expression of amazement. He walked up to Mr. Little and handed him the biohazard bag.

"He told me everything," the boy said, placing his hand on Mr. Little's shoulder.

Mr. Little smiled and nodded. "Good. Nice work, Jacob. You're free to go."

"Thank you," the boy said, as though Mr. Little had just given him a gift.

Chris closed off the partition. Clearly, the experiment was starting to work for some people, but when he checked the progress in his petri dish, he couldn't see any significant change. It was still just his old baby tooth submerged in a puddle of Faz-Goo.

HE TOLD ME EVERYTHING

What if my experiment doesn't work? Chris wondered. *What if I fail?*

Ever since middle school, when his class visited the high school science fair and Chris saw the amazing experiments conducted by Mr. Little's students, Chris had dreamed of being in Science Club. What if he didn't belong there? What if he lacked the necessary knowledge and skill? So many of the Science Club kids were the sons and daughters of scientists themselves, or of doctors or lawyers or college professors. Chris was the son of a clerk and a laborer. Maybe he wasn't of the right stock to make the grade in this intellectual environment.

Suddenly Chris felt drained, depleted. Maybe this meant the Faz-Goo was draining him of the energy it needed to make the experiment work. Or maybe it was just the feeling of him giving up hope. Either way, he was exhausted. He lay down on the cot again and fell asleep instantly.

Chris woke up groggy with his face in a puddle of his own drool. His surroundings were strangely quiet—no whispering, no sounds of movement. He sat up and wiped away the drool. The tendril on his index finger reminded him to check his experiment's progress. Maybe it was finally working. He tried to muster up some hope.

The goo had outgrown the petri dish. It didn't look

like a mouth or much of anything else, really. It was a pink blob, slimy and unpleasant, about the size of a baby's fist.

It was something, anyway. He just wasn't sure what.

Around him, the room was still quiet. Had everybody else left?

After a few seconds, Chris heard rustling, then footsteps, then a voice saying, "He told me everything," followed by Mr. Little's praise and permission for the student to go.

Chris sighed and sat on the cot and waited. He watched the mass in the petri dish, but if there was any progress, it was too slow to see. It was akin to watching paint dry or grass grow.

"Permission to enter?" a voice said from outside the partition.

"Sure," Chris said.

Mr. Little stepped into the cubicle. "How's it going, Chris?"

"Uh . . . I'm not sure, to be honest. Am I the last person left?"

Mr. Little smiled. "No, there are a few other stragglers. I'm just making the rounds and checking up on everybody's progress." He nodded in the direction of the table. "May I?"

"Of course." Chris felt nervous for Mr. Little to look at his nowhere-near-finished project.

Mr. Little approached the table and looked at

the blob, cocking his head in a way that reminded Chris of the family dog. "Hmm," Mr. Little said, leaning down and squinting over the petri dish. "Very curious."

"Did I do something wrong?" Chris asked. He knew where he had gone wrong, even though he wouldn't admit it to Mr. Little. He should have followed directions and pulled out one of his own teeth on the spot like the rest of the students did. He had taken the easy way out because he was a coward, and now he was reaping the consequences.

"As experiments go, this one is pretty impossible to mess up," Mr. Little said, rubbing his chin. "You did put one of your teeth in there, didn't you?"

"Yes, sir," Chris said, not elaborating on the age or origin of the tooth.

"Well, sometimes in science we just have to admit that we don't know why things are happening as they are. The way I see it, Chris, you've got two choices. You can end the experiment and say it just didn't turn out for whatever reason, dispose of whatever that thing is that you've got there, and go home and play video games or whatever it is you do on your own time." He smiled. "Or you can acknowledge that something interesting is happening here, even if we don't quite know what it is, and give it some more time to see what happens."

Chris didn't have to ask himself which choice a real

scientist would make. "I'd like to give it some more time if that's okay."

Mr. Little smiled and clapped him on the back. "It's more than okay! I admire your patience. It's an excellent quality for a scientist to have. Most scientific endeavors worth doing require a great deal of patience and determination." He looked back at the blob. "And to be honest, I'm glad you made that choice because I'm pretty curious to see how this turns out myself." He gave Chris a little two-fingered salute. "I'll check back later, okay?"

"Okay. Thank you, sir."

Chris felt relieved. He had made the right choice, and he had received Mr. Little's approval. Maybe he could be a real Science Club member after all. He sat down to wait because that's what scientists did.

After a while, there was more movement and rustling, followed by similar words uttered by different voices:

"He told me everything."

"She told me everything."

"He told me everything."

Each time, there was Mr. Little's approval for the student to leave.

And then there was silence.

Finally, feeling like the last person on earth, Chris called, "Mr. Little?"

"Yes, Chris?"

"Am I the only one left?"

"You are." His tone was pleasant. "No worries, though."

"Should I give up so you can go home?" Chris wondered if Mr. Little had a wife and some little Littles waiting on him, wondering why the lock-in was taking so long.

Mr. Little poked his head inside the cubicle. "Of course not! I've got no place else to be, and if you're willing to wait, so am I." He grinned and gave a thumbs-up. "Patience and determination."

Once Mr. Little had disappeared from view, Chris felt another wave of exhaustion. Hoping that the energy draining from him was being funneled into the little pink blob, he lay back down on the cot and lost consciousness immediately.

When he awoke, he gasped at the sight on the table. The mass had more than quintupled in size and was now far too large to fit into the biohazard bag. It was still slimy and pink, but it was no longer an inert blob. Shaped somewhat like a limbless human torso, it was now pulsing with life.

Chris felt excited but also a little fearful as he approached his creation. The way it expanded and contracted made him feel like something might jump out of it like a creature he saw in a horror movie once.

He stood over the pulsing mass. Its skin, if you could call it that, was a translucent pink, like a bubble blown from bubble gum. Beneath it was the source of the pulsing, a cluster of baglike structures that were beating to a rhythm that seemed strangely familiar, though Chris didn't know why.

Chris looked at the tendril, now thicker and stronger, that connected him to the newly formed organism on the table. The tendril pulsed in unison with the strange thing's organs. Chris gasped when he realized why the pattern of this pulsing seemed so familiar.

The thing's organs and the tendril that connected him to it were throbbing with the beat of Chris's own heart.

A shudder ran through him, and he was overcome with a sudden need to empty his bladder. Now that he thought about it, he realized he hadn't gone to the bathroom for hours, not since right after the school dismissal bell rang. This knowledge increased his sense of urgency.

But how could he manage to go down the hall to the boys' restroom when he was physically connected to this big, weird, seemingly living thing? He wondered how the other kids had managed it. They probably hadn't needed to go in the first place because they had completed the experiment so much more quickly than he had. Plus, their experiments hadn't yielded something so large and unwieldy.

Just as Chris decided that he was desperate enough to call for Mr. Little and make the pathetic confession that he needed to use the restroom but didn't know how, the pressure in his bladder disappeared. He looked over at the thing on the table, which expelled a large amount of fluid that hit the floor with a splash.

Was that his pee? And what was it doing over there?

Chris knew he should have been embarrassed—he was pretty sure he had just peed on the floor of his science classroom, after all, a big no-no if there ever was one—but mostly he was just confused. Wasn't his pee supposed to come out of his own body? He looked at the tendril. Now even thicker and stronger, it was a tube connecting his body to the thing, feeding it like the umbilical cord that connects a mother with her unborn baby. Maybe his pee had traveled from him through the tube to be expelled by the thing on the table? But why?

He watched the thing pulse some more. Whatever it was, he didn't like it, and he didn't like being connected to it. He didn't like knowing he was letting it leech his energy so it could grow bigger and stronger while he grew more exhausted and weak.

It was time to cut the cord.

The problem was . . . he didn't have anything to cut it with.

He looked around the almost-empty cubicle and spotted the unused pliers. They weren't as good as a knife or a strong pair of scissors, but they were still better than trying to sever the cord with his bare hands. He would use the pliers to grip and squeeze the cord, then give it a hard yank to tear it apart and break the connection.

He poised the pliers to grab the tendril just above where it connected with his left index finger. Then he squeezed.

It felt like somebody was choking the life out of him. Pinching the tube cut off his air supply somehow, and he fell to the floor gasping, landing in a puddle of what was most certainly his own urine. He released the tendril from the pliers, and his breath started to come back. He was too light-headed to get up quickly, so he lay on the wet floor for a few minutes, panting like an overheated dog.

Was there no way to end the connection between him and the disturbing result of his experiment? Or were he and his creation bound together like conjoined twins who shared a vital organ?

He pulled himself up and willed himself to look at the mass on the table. The torso had lengthened, and small pink buds were visible where the arms and legs should have been. Somehow, while he hadn't been watching it, a neck and a head had formed.

The head was hairless, featureless, horrifying.

Chris backed away slowly, bumping into the cot. He didn't want to look at the thing anymore, but he couldn't look away, either. It radiated a horrible fascination, like a gory accident on the side of the highway. He sat on the cot and looked at it until he realized his vision had become blurry and indistinct. It was strange. He had never had trouble with his eyes before.

He put his hand over his right eye, and suddenly it was like the world had been plunged into blackness. He reached up to put his hand over his left eye, and what he found there made him cry out in terror.

His left eye was gone.

It was impossible, of course. The loss of red blood cells and his level of anxiety must have been disrupting his perceptions, making him paranoid, maybe even making him hallucinate. He reached up for his left eye again, but felt only the gaping, empty socket.

Impossible, he told himself again, but then he looked at the tendril. Inside the translucent tube, an orb traveled away from Chris and toward the evolving pink form on the table. The orb was being pushed along by the tendril's pulsations. It was the size and shape of a human eyeball.

What the—

Chris's hand shot up to where his eyeball used to be. There was a popping sound, like a cork being pulled from a bottle, and when Chris looked over at the thing on the table, it was looking back at him with Chris's left eye. The face was no longer featureless. It was now cycloptic.

Chris knew the creature wouldn't be content to stay a cyclops for long. It would be coming for his other eye. And for more parts of him as well.

Even without the benefit of having both of his eyes, Chris could see things clearly now. The organs that throbbed beneath the creature's translucent skin were his organs. Or they used to be.

He was being used as a living organ donor for this thing.

But he wouldn't be a *living* donor for much longer. With his vital organs being siphoned through the tube one by one, he couldn't have much time left.

Chris pulled on the tendril, trying to rip it from his body. But it was connected as solidly as his fingers were to his hand, and gripping the tube constricted it and made him lose his breath. He tried to get up, with a vague, hopeless thought of running to where he could get help, even if it meant dragging the thing behind him like a broken kite on a string. But he found himself too weak to stand.

But he still had his voice, didn't he?

There was nothing to do but scream.

"Help!" he yelled with a voice that was thinner and weaker than he would have liked it to be. "Help! Mr. Little! Anybody! I'm over here! Help me!"

His cries for help were met with silence. Now that all the other students had gone home, had Mr. Little gone home, too? Would he have left without saying goodbye, without giving Chris permission to leave as well?

Chris could not remember ever having felt so utterly alone.

HE TOLD ME EVERYTHING

The yelling had tired him out. Everything tired him out. His muscles felt nonexistent, and his arms and legs were as floppy as overcooked noodles. He sank down on the cot. He needed to think of a plan, a way to escape, but weakness and fatigue overtook him. He didn't mean to fall asleep, but he wasn't strong enough to fight the wave of exhaustion that swept over him.

When he awoke, he opened his one eye and saw the thing sitting on the edge of the table across from him.

Except it wasn't just a thing anymore. It was a boy—a boy who, except for a strangely pink skin tone—looked exactly like Chris. It was Chris's height and build, with his sandy-brown hair. It was wearing Chris's clothes and looking at Chris with what had once been his left eye.

Did that mean Chris was naked? He looked down at his reclining body and quickly saw that it didn't have enough structural integrity to support clothes. Chris's body was devoid of muscles and bone. He was a mass, a blob. He had no idea how he could still be alive, how he could still be aware with so little of him left. There was no way he could hold out much longer.

Chris understood that he would never see his mom and dad and Emma again. He would never take another bike ride to the Dairy Bar and the lake with Josh and Kyle. Somebody else would have to take Porkchop for his walks and feed him his dinner.

The thing got down from the table and used Chris's bones and muscles to walk over to the cot.

With his one remaining eye, Chris saw his creation. He saw that this creature looked so much like him that nobody would ever know the difference. It would go to Chris's house and take its place in Chris's family. It would sit at the dinner table with his mom and dad and Emma, eating hot dogs and macaroni and cheese. It would play with Porkchop. It would study at Cool Beans Coffee and go to school and Science Club meetings.

Chris saw that his own life was going to go on without him.

Chris struggled to speak. His throat and mouth were as parched as a desert, and he was pretty sure his lips were gone. It was hard to make himself heard.

"Listen." His voice finally came out as a croak. "My mom and dad—they're going to love you because they love me. Be nice to them." He stopped to try to catch his breath. Breathing used to be so easy he never even thought about it. "Be nice to my sister, too. She's a good kid. A Girl Scout. She's your sister now." The words were hard to get out, but he had more he needed to say. "Mrs. Thomas, our neighbor. She's old. She's a nice lady. Help her when you can. And play with Porkchop."

The creature furrowed its brow, looking confused. "I am to play . . . with a porkchop?"

Chris felt the last of his strength fading. He whispered, "Porkchop is my dog. Yours . . . now." Chris felt the tendril that connected him to his life disintegrating. "Take care of him," he said, but his words came out so softly he was afraid that only he could hear them.

Chris felt a strange sensation of suction where his right eye was, and then everything went black. He listened as his eyeball was sucked through the tube. There were more slurping sounds, too, as other parts of him were drawn up through the tendril. Parts he knew he couldn't live without. It was like the creature was drinking him, sucking the last of his organs through a long straw, like the dregs of a milkshake, leaving only an empty vessel.

Chris, as the creature would have to learn to call itself, stood over the shapeless mass of empty flesh on the cot. He opened the biohazard bag and stuffed the fleshy remains of the experiment inside of it. He was surprised that he was able to cram all of it into one bag, and when he picked it up, the contents were surprisingly light.

It left the cubicle and found Mr. Little sitting at his desk drinking from a Styrofoam cup of coffee and munching on a doughnut. "Well, good morning, Chris!" Mr. Little said, standing up and brushing crumbs from his mustache. "You had a long night, didn't you? But don't keep me in suspense. Did you finally complete the experiment? Did you get the results you wanted?"

The new Chris's eyes were wide and full of wonder. Soon he would be stepping out of the classroom and out of the school and into the world for the first time.

Chris handed the biohazard bag to Mr. Little. He

looked into the teacher's eyes and smiled. "He told me everything," he said.

As Chris walked outside the school building, the sun was warm on his face. The sky was blue, the clouds were white and fluffy, and birds chirped in the trees. Chris smiled. It was a beautiful day.

ABOUT THE AUTHORS

Scott Cawthon is the author of the bestselling video game series *Five Nights at Freddy's*, and while he is a game designer by trade, he is first and foremost a storyteller at heart. He is a graduate of The Art Institute of Houston and lives in Texas with his family.

Andrea Rains Waggener is an author, novelist, ghostwriter, essayist, short story writer, screenwriter, copywriter, editor, poet, and a proud member of Kevin Anderson & Associates' team of writers. In a past she prefers not to remember much, she was a claims adjuster, JCPenney's catalogue order-taker (before computers!), appellate court clerk, legal writing instructor, and lawyer. Writing in genres that vary from her chick-lit novel, *Alternate Beauty*, to her dog how-to book, *Dog Parenting*, to her self-help book, *Healthy, Wealthy, and Wise*, to ghostwritten memoirs to ghostwritten YA, horror, mystery, and mainstream fiction projects, Andrea still manages to find time to watch the rain and obsess over her dog and her knitting, art, and music projects. She lives with her husband and said dog on the Washington Coast, and if she isn't at home creating something, she can be found walking on the beach.

Elley Cooper writes fiction for young adults and adults. She has always loved horror and is grateful to Scott Cawthon for letting her spend time in his dark and twisted universe. Elley lives in Tennessee with her family and many spoiled pets and can often be found writing books with Kevin Anderson & Associates.

Larson heard it before he saw it.

And when he did hear it, he couldn't believe how it had managed to form behind him without him hearing it. The sounds were ear-splitting.

Larson's initial thought was that a train was barreling down on him. The clatter, rumble, blast, and shriek that now made him whirl around defied his ability to process the noise.

He had no better success with what he was seeing.

But he couldn't even try to process that. He just ran.

Barreling out of the shelter of the factory, leaving his sedan and the garbage bag behind, Larson raced toward the dock. Realizing it provided no cover, he veered back toward the building, to the overhang that sheltered an old forklift. Crouching next to the forklift, he peeked into the factory.

Yep. He wasn't going mad—he'd seen what he thought he'd seen. But it hadn't started chasing him yet. It seemed to still be deciding what form to take. It continued to coalesce into the most abominable thing Larson had ever encountered.

Still a little disoriented from his battle with the rabbit creature and his temporarily compressed state, Jake wanted only to curl up and sleep someplace safe. He was so tired.

But he couldn't rest yet. The man Jake had seen earlier—the detective—was nearby, and he was in trouble.

As soon as Jake climbed out of the trash compactor, he had full awareness of what was going on in the factory. Part of his awareness came from "normal" senses—he could *see* the trash monster building itself up larger and larger. He could *hear* the clanking, thumping, and clattering of metal latching onto metal. The rest of his awareness, however, came from something he didn't understand. He just *knew* the detective was nearby and was in terrible danger.

Jake also knew something else. He knew *he* was in danger, too.

Completely against his will, Jake's metal body began to skim across the concrete toward the trash-being. It felt like Jake was caught in an alien spaceship's tractor beam . . . except he wasn't being towed into the sky; he was being sucked into the horrible metal man-thing.

Jake immediately put all his strength into fighting the pull. After just a few seconds, he was able to stop his forward motion. Around him, animatronic parts and trash whizzed past and glommed onto the massive body forming from the garbage. Jake, though, stayed fast, committing himself to remaining separate from the evil entity. And because he was Jake—a boy who tried to help anyone who needed it—he also extended his intention to the other animatronic debris being vacuumed up by the junkyard fiend. He did all he could to save the other parts from falling under the thing's control.

He'd managed to hold back a few arms and legs and joints and screws, but suddenly he felt the resistance of mangled, metallic skeletal remains. Something was fighting against him; it wanted to be absorbed by the whole.

Jake managed to keep himself planted as he turned to see what had enough self-awareness that it could choose to join the bulging trash being. For a few seconds, the debris roiling around him remained locked in chaotic movement, but then he spied a battered, rusting, vaguely female-shaped endoskeleton with a long neck crawling away from the other rubbish.

Jake immediately tried to reach whatever was controlling the girl-endoskeleton. *Let me save you*, he called to her with his mind.

At first, he got no response, but then his mind was filled with the sound of high-pitched laughter. It was a creepy cackling that skittered through his whole being.

Before Jake could react to the sound—and whatever it meant—the girl-endoskeleton's crawl turned into a disturbingly quick slither. Scraping across the floor, the girl-endoskeleton shot toward Jake.

Jake's inner resources were a little played-out, given that he was still fighting the tug of the trash monster. So he could do little to resist when the girl-endoskeleton suddenly sprang off the ground and hit him full-on, knocking him to the ground.

Jake couldn't feel the impact, of course, but it still stunned him. For a few seconds, he couldn't move. He found himself eye-to-eye with a corroded face whose mouth was stretched into a poisonous smile that looked anything but friendly.

The smile supercharged Jake's need to get free. He immediately tried to throw off his attacker.

But she didn't budge. Instead, she pinned him with extraordinary strength, and her round, animatronic eyes started to glow white-hot. The glaring light began to bore through Jake's doll eyes, searing into him, reaching deep inside.

The moment the light drilled into him, Jake felt the same evil he'd fought in the trash compactor. Only this evil felt stronger, like it was the core of what Jake had sensed in the things Andrew had infected.

Jake also felt something else; some of that badness was inside of him! He hadn't noticed it before, but now it was unmistakable. A piece of the evil he'd battled—cold and cruel—had been hiding in Jake's spirit. Just as it had hitched a ride in Andrew, it had apparently burrowed its way into Jake as well.

Jake didn't like having the nasty girl-endoskeleton so close to him, but he was happy for her to take away the yuck he could feel within him. It was leaving now, returning to its source; the girl-thing drawing the energy out of him with her burning gaze.

Jake felt it the instant the evil left him, but even if he hadn't felt it, he'd have known. The girl-endoskeleton looked somehow brighter now, less rusty. Taking back that part of her had made her stronger.

As if acknowledging Jake's awareness, the girl-thing cocked her metal skull and winked at him. It was a slow-motion wink filled with what looked like gleeful triumph. Then the girl-endoskeleton let go of Jake and flew backward, allowing herself to be absorbed into the horrid metal giant.

Mesmerized by the bizarre osmosis of robotic parts—including one full female-shaped endoskeleton that had attacked the Stitchwraith before releasing itself to the trash amalgamation—Larson hadn't managed to move from where he hid. Now, however, the trash-thing took a step forward . . . and it stared right at Larson.

The moment the rabbit-shaped fusion of trash met Larson's gaze, Larson was able to accept what he'd known when he'd first watched the monster put itself together. The thing was Afton.

Even though the rabbit was made up of disturbingly arranged animatronic parts and was twice a normal man's size, it exuded William Afton's unmistakable energy. In a way, the patchwork face resembled photos Larson had seen of the serial killer, as if Afton had the power to shape other material into his own countenance.

Afton's Amalgamation took another step forward.

Larson, appalled by his stupid inaction, muttered, "Crap." He looked around. If he ran now, he could slip between the next building to the north and get away.

But . . .

He looked beyond the immediate buildings and the lake. This district was surrounded by old neighborhoods, the kind of neighborhoods with two-story houses, gnarled oak trees . . . and children.

Ryan's voice spoke in his head: "Teacher says dads are like superheroes. But you're not. Superheroes don't break promises."

Ryan was right. Superheroes didn't break promises, and Larson wanted to be Ryan's superhero. Today, he could do that by keeping his promise to the city, his promise to protect and serve. He was not going to run away.

He had to stop this thing before it got out.

But how?

Larson looked around. He catalogued what he saw: The factory currently incubating a creature from the underworld. Dock and lake behind the factory. An empty field to the left of the factory, beyond which lay houses in which little boys like his Ryan were playing video games, building forts, doing homework, or wishing their dads were at home.

How could he fight something powered by such evil?

Before he could answer that question, the creature that looked like both a man-shaped pile of junk and a deformed rabbit turned and went deeper into the factory. What was it doing?

Larson crept out from behind the forklift and sidled through the entryway. Reaching his sedan, he crouched and listened. He noticed the bag of parts he'd left on the ground by his open driver's side door. He grabbed the bag. He had a feeling he might need it.

Inside the building, the thing crunched and huffed. Looping the bag around his wrist as he'd done earlier, Larson ran toward the sound.

Although following the sound was easy, understanding it was harder. The noises Larson was hearing kept changing. Maybe they shifted when the thing's parts shifted.

Sometimes the sound was a chittering noise. Sometimes it was a crackle. Sometimes it was the fingernails-on-a-chalkboard caterwaul of metal being torn from metal. It was always something that made Larson forget to breathe.

But he didn't stop moving. He couldn't.

Following the sounds, he went past the trash compacting room and found himself in a wide hallway. A series of what looked like storage rooms or equipment rooms opened up off the hallway. From the now squalling and skidding sounds ahead of him, he knew he was going in the right direction. The skidding devolved into a snarling wet popping sound. It reminded Larson of the autopsies he sometimes had to attend. A corpse made a similar sound when its ribcage was being parted and its organs were being removed. Larson felt his stomach turn against the roast beef sandwich he'd had for lunch, but he commanded the sandwich to stay where it was.

The hallway turned a corner, and Larson hesitated. He waited until the squishy taps moved farther away from him. Then he sidled around the corner.

The second he looked ahead, he almost turned and ran.

Hulking shadows skated along the walls of the hallway in front of him. The shadows, like the rabbit monster, were in perpetual motion. They rose and fell, billowed and contracted. They looked alive, and for all Larson knew, they were.

No matter. He had to go on.

Larson took another step.

And another.

Afton's Amalgamation crashed through the interior wall of the hallway.

Larson attempted to leap forward to clear the thing's line of sight, but he wasn't fast enough. He had just a second, if that, to register the appalling composite of animatronic body parts and faces that came at him with the speed of a race car and the force of a battering ram. Did he just see an eye on a kneecap? And was that kneecap where a shoulder should have been? Had feet been protruding from the thing's neck? And did the feet have mouths? How many mouths had he just seen? Dozens?

He didn't have time to answer any of these questions before he was hurled not just into, but *through* the other hallway wall. Aware of only pain as he flew through the air, he collided with something hard, and then he felt nothing.

As soon as the trash monster had integrated the girl-endoskeleton, it had turned away and clomped into the factory's interior. It hadn't given Jake even a glance as it had passed him. It apparently had enough parts to be satisfied.

For a few seconds after the metal man-thing had disappeared from Jake's view, Jake considered running away. But he couldn't. The detective was still here. And he was still in danger. Jake had to help.

So Jake made himself get up and follow the monster. It wasn't hard to do. It was making a racket. Jake ran toward the sound.

Piercing jabs of light stabbed at the blackness that surrounded Larson. He squeezed his eyes shut and moaned. Why couldn't he be left in peace?

His head pounded. Touching his forehead, he felt a knot above his left eyebrow, and his fingers came away wet. His chest and his side throbbed, too. He was sure he'd cracked a rib or two, maybe more. He felt warm wetness at his side. Maybe he did more than crack a rib. Maybe he broke one and it pierced his skin. Or maybe something sharp had cut him. He was barely aware of leaning against something jagged and hard. Some kind of equipment? Maybe he'd been cut on that.

Voices whispered at him in the dark. Their words capered around the flashes of light in his head. He screwed up his forehead, both to combat the throbbing pain in his skull and to help him focus on what the words meant.

He suddenly remembered how he got into this place of darkness and light, of pain and whispering voices. Afton's Amalgamation.

He stiffened. Where was it?

"Hurry." That was one of the words in his head.

Or were the words *in* his head? Were they outside his head? If they were outside his head, where were they coming from?

It sounded like children whispering. Or did it? His left ear burned like he'd been slapped hard on the side of the head. His right ear felt like it was filled with cotton. The whispers rose and fell. He could see the words in his mind like ballet dancers spinning and leaping and dipping.

Then three words joined together in perfect choreography. "Open your eyes," they said.

Larson did.

Afton was standing over him. So close. Too close.

Larson looked into the enormous face hovering above his own. It was a face of nightmares. With eyes made of metal sockets and spark plugs, a mouth formed from long pistons, and cheekbones composed of large gears and bolts, the face seemed to be held together with bits of pointed metal, rusted pipes, and what appeared to be actual bone . . . but not the bones one would expect to see in a face. An animatronic elbow acting as a chin was attached with a rat skeleton, and a brow made from part of a motor was affixed by a bird's foot.

As repulsive as all of this was, though, it wasn't the metal junk that sent chills skittering down Larson's spine. The truly repugnant thing about Afton's new face was that it was . . . in motion. Tucked in and around the metal scrap and bone, animatronic parts wriggled and writhed. And they were singing, or at least that's what it sounded like. Larson could hear a harmonized chorus; various parts of it seemed to be coming from Afton's spinning ankle-joint nose, shimmying shoulder-socket forehead, and tapping metal-footed jaws.

Each of Afton's ears was made of a different animatronic part. One ear was three-quarters of a metal hand, and the other ear was a metal jaw. Both the hand and the jaw were moving in time to the music, which seemed to be snippets from the old floor shows the Freddy's animatronics used to do.

Thankfully, Larson didn't have time to examine Afton's makeshift face any further, because Afton's Amalgamation raised a hand that was actually a foot and a hip joint. Larson lunged to his right, but he wasn't fast enough. The sharp metal toes of the foot Afton was using as a hand impaled Larson's belly.

Larson cried out when hot pain shot through his gut and radiated across his entire torso, but he was able to jerk free and stagger out of the hideous thing's reach. Grabbing his lower belly, Larson felt warmth flow from between his fingers, down over his right hipbone as he busted out of the room he'd been thrown into and ran down the hall to the south exit of the warehouse.

Jake watched the detective flee down the hall. He called out, but the detective didn't hear him.

Jake was mad at himself. If he hadn't hesitated after the girl-endoskeleton attacked him, he could have gotten to the detective in time to prevent what had just happened. But Jake had been weak and selfish. As a result, he'd been too late.

The detective would know, of course, that he'd been stabbed, but he'd think that was all that had happened. He would think the injury was bad, but what he didn't know was that the injury itself wasn't the problem. The problem was that when the trash monster stabbed the detective, it infected him with the spirit of the horrible man who animated it.

Jake had known that the evil junk demon was controlled by the awful thing that had wanted Andrew. Spirits, Jake had discovered, possessed something that was similar to a smell. Each one was distinct.

This particular spirit smelled really, really bad. And when it had stabbed the detective, the smell had gone into the detective's body. Jake was afraid the detective had been infected, and he didn't know exactly how bad the infection would be. Pretty bad, was his guess. For sure, Afton's spirit would fill the detective with evil. But what if it did more than that? What if it killed him? Jake had to get the infection out.

The metal monster thundered past Jake, again paying no attention to him. The monster was intent on catching the detective, so Jake chased after it.

Behind Larson, Afton's Amalgamation howled like a demented hound from hell. Larson could hear its ponderous steps pursing him as he ran, each footfall sounding like a thunderclap, each thunderclap louder than the last.

If Afton had been breathing, Larson would have felt that breath on his neck as he threw his shoulder into the closed door and fell out into the dwindling daylight. He turned and ran north along the side of the factory. He knew where he needed to go next, but he might or might not make it.

He ignored his pain and ran as fast as he could.

The second after Larson got where he was going, Afton

ripped a hole in the side of the building to pursue the detective. Larson heard the clamorous rending of metal and Afton's bawling shout. Then he heard the singing he'd heard earlier. It was louder now, almost frantic, as if the cannibalized animatronic parts were trying to comfort themselves with music.

Larson imagined the amalgamation's unholy head rotating this way and that, looking for Larson. As Larson did what he needed to do next, he hoped Afton's current form had no supernatural powers other than its ability to animate junk. If Afton was telepathic, Larson was screwed. But he had to try.

To Larson's amazement, he was able to get to the forklift without Afton being aware of it. As he climbed onto the driver's seat, Larson hefted the bag of parts he'd been carrying around. He started to tuck the bag onto the floorboard by his feet, but suddenly, its contents started moving.

For a moment, Larson forgot all about the trash rabbit because not only was the bag moving, but voices were coming from inside it, too. Holding his breath, Larson gingerly opened the bag.

As soon as the bag opened, the voices got louder. Larson gasped and jerked his hand back.

The last thing Larson had put in this bag was a mask. The mask was cracked and muddied, but its features were clear. With rosy red cheeks and purple stripes that stretched from the bottom of its hollow black eyes to the top of its wide-open mouth, red lipstick highlighting an amplified pucker, the mask could have been amusing. But it wasn't—especially now, because now the mask had come alive. Its mouth was wide open, and it was wailing something unintelligible.

Larson didn't need to understand its cries, though.

Larson kept his foot smashed against the forklift's accelerator.

Afton, however, wasn't going into the lake without a fight. He planted his hand/jaw/joint–constructed feet and leaned into the forklift. Larson's forward progress slowed. But it didn't stop. He dug in. "Come on," he urged the machine. "Come on."

The machine gave a great grumble and surged forward. Afton was pushed to the very edge of the dock.

"Go, go, go, go," Larson muttered, his gaze locked on Afton's soul-freezing eye sockets.

Afton was almost at the edge. He was going to . . .

Pieces of the forklift began peeling away and flying through the air toward Afton. First the mast, then the lift cylinder, then the backrest. One after the other, parts of the forklift disconnected from the whole and swept toward Afton's Amalgamation.

The tilt cylinder, the wheels, the overhead guard—they went in quick succession, followed by the fork's prongs. Everything was being absorbed into Afton's merger of metal, plastic, and wire.

Larson watched in frightened awe when even the evidence he'd hung on the front of the forklift got slurped into Afton's continually evolving construction. He thought he saw one black-and-white-striped arm get siphoned up into Afton's left leg. Then the steering wheel was snatched from his grasp, and he felt the operator's seat gyrate under him.

Larson jumped off the forklift, and fell to the dock. Holding his gut again, he began crawling backward, away from Afton's macabre evolution. It continued to consume the forklift.

Within seconds, the forklift was nearly gone. Just a few pieces of battered yellow metal remained. The rest was wriggling through Afton's crevices, joining with a jaw here, a gear there.

The monster lifted its face to Larson. The detective had nowhere to hide now, and he wouldn't make it far with his injuries. He had one trick left: stalling.

"Afton?" Larson asked. "That is you in there, isn't it? Though I'm not even sure what to call you now."

Afton's Amalgamation glared back at the detective. Repositioning his pieces so he stood taller and broader on the end of the dock, the loathsome atrocity that was William Afton announced in such sonorous tones that the dock juddered, "I am Agony."

Larson felt his lip curl. He said nothing. But his mouth dropped open when all the faces and mouths on Afton's trash-body began talking at once. No, not talking. It was the singing again.

Larson hadn't had time to examine all of the Afton behemoth when he got up-close-and-personal with Afton's jigsaw-puzzle face, so Larson hadn't noticed then whether the totality of Afton's junk had been part of the mutant stage show he'd glimpsed. But now he could see that every animatronic part crammed into Afton's warped configuration was doing its best to sing and dance. All over Afton, animatronic arms and legs, hands and feet, and fingers and toes were swaying and bopping to the music the mouths were attempting to perform.

Goosebumps erupted on Larson's skin. He covered his ears, then, disgusted with himself for letting the creep-show unnerve him. He groaned, got up on one knee, and then pushed himself into an upright, standing position. He faced Afton.

"Enough!" Larson shouted.

The voices stopped. The animatronic parts went still.

Larson closed his eyes and took a deep breath. He was preparing himself for what he thought might be his final battle.

Jake had caught up with the rabbit-shaped trash monster just as the detective had attacked it with the forklift. Not sure how to help at that point, Jake had just hung back and watched as the forklift had driven the monster closer and closer to the lake.

When the forklift began coming apart, Jake still wasn't sure what to do. He was thinking hard, though. He figured that at the very least, if the trash rabbit got the upper hand, Jake could charge over and pick up the detective. Maybe he could carry the man to safety before the monster could catch them.

While Jake was thinking this through, though, something strange happened. The instant the detective closed his eyes, the girl-endoskeleton separated herself from the rest of the trash rabbit's parts.

Undulating past an arm, a leg, and a hip joint, the girl-endoskeleton wormed her way to the outer layer of the trash rabbit, and she leaped away from him. As soon as she launched herself free, Jake pressed back into the shadows. He didn't want another encounter with the girl-thing. She was scary.

Tense enough that he'd have been holding his breath if he actually breathed, Jake watched the girl-endoskeleton wriggle across the dock. He kept his gaze riveted on her until he saw her slink toward a gaping vent opening in the side of the factory.

When Larson opened his eyes, he expected Afton would still be glaring at him. But Afton wasn't looking at Larson at all. He was staring past Larson intently, almost pleadingly.

Larson turned to see what Afton was looking at, and he saw what appeared to be a female-shaped metal endoskeleton disappearing into a vent opening—it seemed to be the same endoskeleton he'd seen before. Larson frowned. He returned his gaze to Afton . . . and he saw the plea dissolve into despair. Afton was still a horrifying synthesis of scrap, but he'd taken on an eerily human-looking demeanor. In spite of its size, Afton's mountain of metal seemed to shrink inward, as if becoming weak and frail. Afton's visage now looked lost and defeated. Afton's Amalgamation dropped its head, and then Afton's expression shifted into what could have been puzzlement.

Larson refocused, and he immediately could see what Afton was looking at. Afton was staring at his right side, where the purple-striped mask from the bag was congealed to the animatronic parts. The mask was no longer wailing as it had been when Larson had last seen it. It's white face now looked satisfied, victorious.

Larson watched, amazed, as Afton's Amalgamation started

to pull itself apart. Or, at least, that's what appeared to be happening.

The destruction started with an arm embedded in the animated junk heap's shoulder. The arm reached out and grabbed a gear-shaped cheekbone. Wrenching the cheekbone from the face, the arm moved on to the ear made from a jaw.

Another arm came loose from what was a thigh. It reached for the gear that made up a kneecap. It unscrewed it then flung it into the lake.

Now another two arms reached out. One grabbed the piston-constructed lips. The other removed an ear-shaped elbow.

And more arms began to move. They seemed to spout from every part of Afton's metal jumble like oil gushers shoving through the earth's surface. Every arm that came out grabbed something. One piece after the other was plucked by reaching fingers. It took only a minute before Afton's Amalgamation was a roiling lump of body parts and connective pieces.

Then unidentifiable fluids begin spilling from the deconstructing trash. As they flowed, Afton stumbled backward, one short step from the end of the dock.

Larson's legs gave out. He dropped to the deck and sat with both hands pressed to his lower stomach, his eyes wide and staring as blood started pouring from the trash rabbit's mouth.

The blood sluiced over the plastic, metal, bone, and wire, and it mixed with the other fluids to flow like hot tar onto the warped planks of the dock. The once-identifiable, though grotesque, rabbit was becoming a decomposing trash heap, a frail pile of disparate bits, weak and struggling.

When the last piece fell onto the pyramid of waste, Afton screamed, and the entire tower of worthlessness fell back off the dock.

For at least a minute, Larson sat and stared, trying to figure out if he could ever put words to what had just happened. Then, painfully, he stood. On unsteady legs, he took short, slow steps toward the edge of the dock. Taking a deep breath, he looked down at the water.

He'd been prepared to jump back if he had to. But he didn't have to. What remained of Afton wasn't a threat.

Afton was nothing but a floating stain of insignificant parts bobbing on the surface of the lake. Larson relaxed his muscles, but he covered his nose with his hand. The air was heavy with the smells of acid and decomposition. Oily lather skimmed over the water.

Feeling dizzy, Larson leaned against a post at the corner of the dock. He listened to the water fizz and burble. And he watched the parts begin to sink. A leg. An arm. A foot. Gears. Joints. Mouths. The lake swallowed piece after piece until, finally, only one thing remained.

The last piece of Afton's trash-self that the lake slipped down its liquid gullet was the purple-striped mask of the marionette.

Larson crumpled to the dock. And that's when he spotted the Stitchwraith again.

He could feel blood seeping from his wounds, but he ignored it. His vision was becoming blurry; he had to strain to watch the Stitchwraith. As the Stitchwraith stepped out of the shadows and onto the dock, Larson tried to push himself back up onto his feet. He couldn't let Afton walk away from this factory . . . in *any* form.

Jake knew the detective thought that Jake was as bad as the trash rabbit. He could feel the detective's anger and fear.

But that didn't matter. The detective's infection was already starting to spread. Jake had to stop it.

his hands.

And it worked! Jake's metal hand began to glow red with heat. As soon as the glow began to radiate outward, Jake held his hand over the detective's wound.

The detective was barely aware of what was happening, but he cried out and tried to writhe away from Jake's hand. Jake used his other hand to hold the detective in place.

As soon as the detective was still, Jake lowered his glowing hand. The detective screamed in pain, but Jake, wincing, ignored the sound. He had to burn the infection away . . . even if it hurt the detective. As soon as the heat met the detective's skin, a greenish gunk that looked like a revolting cross between spoiled cottage cheese and pistachio pudding bubbled up to the surface. It immediately began sizzling, which created a nasty reek of putrid, decaying flesh. Jake would have wrinkled his nose if his nose could have wrinkled. But he stayed where he was, and he kept his hand in place until the last of the repulsive glop was gone.

By then, the detective had passed out. Jake was happy about that.

Jake looked around. What should he do now?

The shriek of sirens answered that question. He had to leave. Help was coming, and that help wouldn't see Jake as a good guy.

Jake straightened and ran toward the factory. He figured he could wind his way through its interior and escape out the other side. As Jake ducked into a narrow hall, though, his footsteps faltered. He'd just had a horrible realization.

Jake forced himself to keep going as he thought about the trash rabbit and the way it had come apart. Jake's own spirit had been close enough to the awful man controlling the trash rabbit—the detective had called him Afton—to know that the awful man's spirit wasn't as powerful as it had pretended to be. Jake had felt that Afton's spirit was barely hanging onto this reality. So how would Afton have been able to battle the detective the way he did?

Jake reached the far side of the factory. He poked his head out a small door and looked around.

Twilight had given way to darkness. The moon was bright enough to light up the area, but the night created enough shadows for Jake to stay out of sight.

As he fled the factory, Jake faced the truth that he'd just uncovered: Something besides Afton had been controlling the trash rabbit. And whatever it was, it was worse.